CAUGHT BETWEEN

CAUGHT BETWEEN

Shaun G. Seward

Book Guild Publishing
Sussex, England

First published in Great Britain in 2012 by
The Book Guild Ltd
Pavilion View
19 New Road
Brighton, BN1 1UF

Typesetting in Baskerville by
Nat-Type, Cheshire

Printed in Great Britain by
CPI Antony Rowe

A catalogue record for this book is available from
The British Library.

ISBN 978 1 84624 682 1

1

Trouble in the Hero of Waterloo

Sydney

Luke Crooks, twenty-six years old, was casually dressed in a crisp short-sleeved powder-blue Hackett shirt, boot-cut Levis and the latest style of trendy dark-blue Kickers shoes; all top designer clothes, nothing but the best. His dark hair was closely cropped, his sideburns groomed to a thin point. He was a tall, good-looking man, naturally well-built with a killer smile. It had been six months since he had moved to Sydney, and Luke was trying to forget the reasons why he had ended up here. He had fallen for the laid-back Australian way of life; the hot, bright, sunny days, the long, warm leisurely evenings. He certainly didn't miss the grey cold rain of old West London; well, maybe occasionally now and then he would pine for home. He missed his family, particularly his younger brother, for whom he felt so responsible, and his beloved mum, to whom he did not have time to explain why he had to leave so suddenly.

Overall, though, he enjoyed it here in Sydney, much preferring the warm climate, which suited him. He kept a low profile, so nobody really knew him, and neither did he really want anyone to – only Shannon, and she knew only what Luke wanted her to. One day he would have to tell her everything. 'ONE DAY.' However, at this time, nobody there needed to be concerned about his personal history.

But then, out of the blue, Luke had received a phone call.

'Hello, mate, I'm coming to see you,' said a familiar voice. Luke remembered his first reaction: instead of being pleased, he was shocked to hear from his old pal Monks.

'No one is supposed to know where I am,' he'd replied.

'You know I can always find you, mate. I need a little holiday,' Monks said cheerfully.

'When are you coming over?' Luke asked.

'I'm flying out to Sydney on Tuesday. It will be just like the old days.'

'That's what I'm worried about,' he replied, laughing. He did not imagine anything would come of it. Then Luke asked Monks, 'How did you get my number? I am supposed to be in hiding from everyone at home.'

'You're elusive all right, but I caught up with old man Kravis – I thought he might know a thing or two,' Monks replied. He could always find people when he had to. However, this usually meant either that he was in trouble or, even worse, that he was going to bring a lot of grief to somebody else, and that was definitely not good news for Luke.

Now, a week after that call, standing here with his old friend was an unpleasant reminder of why he had to leave London in the first place. It seemed to Luke that his luck was about to desert him.

The look etched onto Monks' face revealed all Luke needed to know, and what was more, everything he wished to avoid. He thought that he had managed to escape from all this type of bullshit a long time ago. The last thing he needed at this stage of his emancipation was for history to repeat itself. Luke could soon be finding himself back where he started, which was somewhere Luke Crooks certainly did not wish to be.

Only a few months ago, Luke could not care less. It was a different era, he never thought of what the consequences may be and he was not at all concerned by what the future may hold. But it was all starting to get out of hand. Were they all bad memories? Luke had just sought after a different life – as it all turned out, he had no choice but to move away. More or less overnight he had vanished into thin air, away from all the people he loved and cared about.

As Luke reminisced, he was monitoring Monks' body language; the signs he was reading were not looking too good, he thought. He remembered the awful sound of grown men wincing, the smell of piss and shit as they soiled themselves and most of all the terror in their eyes, an image he would under no circumstances ever likely be able to forget. It all seemed, well, entertaining to begin with, or so Monks had always persuaded Luke to think. Back in England an evening's entertainment would never be complete without Monks trying, and usually succeeding, to pull somebody in to a fight. All too often this had became an unfortunate occurrence on a night out on the tiles with Monks.

In addition, there was the fact that everybody wanted to be a top boy – we all thought we could be a big shot, thought Luke. All of his peers did, it was just how you grew up – you had to adapt to your environment, though deep down Luke knew this was all one way or another the wrong way to carry on. Once you have a bit of a reputation, and you have earned respect from your peers, the opportunities will open up, or so that's what you were led to believe. This was what Luke had fallen for and then, inevitably, it all went too far.

Looking at Monks now, Luke knew what to expect. He hoped it would turn out fine, but feared that it probably wouldn't. He remembered how they had always stuck together no matter what situation they found themselves in. Since they were kids, Luke Crooks and Marc Crompton were blood brothers, inseparable, always in some scrape or another. Luke had to remember their oath never to let each other down. And up to a point they never had.

2

Moneymaker

England

Six months or so earlier, life was entirely different. West London is a vibrant place. Luke had grown up around there and he knew Shepherd's Bush and its surrounding area like the back of his hand. Furthermore, he loved it. Luke had plenty of good mates, he always managed to have a bird on the go, plus he had a thriving business to boot. Okay, so not all of his business was strictly legit, but it wasn't as if anybody was going to get hurt. The problem with it all was, when you are doing all right for yourself, certain people get to hear about it and try to get a piece of the action. Of course, when your business partner is Marc Crompton, or Monks as he was commonly known, you should be okay.

Luke and Monks were returning from a successful trip down to Maidenhead in Berkshire. They were into stealing mobile telephones, a cracking little moneymaker. When mobile phones came onto the scene, they were among the first people to realise that stealing mobiles for their SIM cards could be worth a small amount of cash. There was always a plentiful selection of top-of-the-range mobile phones all over the south-east of England. On a Friday afternoon, they would pick a town within a 50-mile radius of the capital. Then they would get into Monks' BMW, drive to

5

that particular town and park up in a multi-storey car park from around half past eleven. They would always make sure that they never left the targeted town any later than half past four. That was the golden rule. They would walk from bar to bar and pop into restaurants, keeping a keen eye out for local office workers and suited and booted executives, as they were easy pickings for a couple of clued-up wide boys like these. Ever since they were teenagers Luke and Monks were first-class pickpockets. It was a simple assignment for these two. They would enter an establishment, go to the bar separately and scan the area briefly. Luke would work from one end and Monks from the other and both of them would target three people each. Within five minutes in each pub, bar, or restaurant, when the required amount of phones had been relieved from the stated number of patrons, they would meet up in the middle of the venue, nod to each other, then vacate the premises quickly but gracefully. In a busy market town like Maidenhead, where they had been that day, they could get back to Shepherd's Bush by six o' clock with up to thirty handsets, a few wallets and maybe a couple of hundred quid in cash. Once they had delivered the goods to their trusted fence, they sometimes cleared over £600 each for half a day's pilfering – not a bad little earner, considering the ease of their crime, and they quite enjoyed their pleasant ventures into the country.

This was the start of their ingenious little enterprise; soon enough it came to their knowledge that inside every mobile phone would be a small amount of gold. This moved their con to even more profitable levels, as in countries like China dealers were now starting to pay a small fortune for these mobiles mainly for the gold, plus the electronic components that were inside them. With Luke and Monks collecting and now exporting these phones at such a rate, it was only a matter of time before some of the bigger villains in the parish got to hear all about their excellent side venture. Danny

Chilton was one of these villains. If anybody wanted to know who was making good money on his manor, this was the man, and he was beginning to hear quite a bit about profit in mobile phones. Although Luke enjoyed the buzz of pickpocketing, he knew he could not keep it up forever. He realised that eventually they would have to pack it in. He only intended it to be temporary until he could save up enough money to buy into his uncle's business.

Luke worked part-time in his uncle's shop from Monday to Thursday and the occasional Friday and Saturday. It was a traditional family confectioner-cum-tobacconist's. Not many of these traditional little shops were still trading in London – they were from a bygone age, but Luke's uncle still did a roaring trade. He would start his workday at six in the morning and finish by two in the afternoon. It was not particularly hard work for a fit young man like Luke, but he really enjoyed it. He began to work there at the age of twelve, just after his granddad died. His Uncle Darren inherited the shop, and with no children of his own he always looked after his sister's boys. It started out as a part-time job, but after a few years Luke virtually ran the shop with his Uncle Darren, whom he looked up to as a real father figure.

Uncle Darren was always around when Luke and his younger brother Mickey were small; he hated their errant father, who was constantly knocking their mother Julie about and used to give the kids a good hiding every now and then. More than once Darren had to come round to sort out the drunken bully but, being the cowardly bastard he was, their father would usually disappear for a while after handing out one of his random beatings. Darren did manage to catch hold of him one time, only for Julie to beg him not to hurt him, as she believed he could change to be a good husband and dad to the boys. Of course, he bluffed his way out of a kicking. For appearances he would behave himself for a month, only to return to his handy ways with them all. If it were not for Julie's forgiving nature, Darren would probably have killed the bastard. Mind you, they did get rid of the useless piece of shit – soon after Luke turned sixteen, he and his Uncle Darren managed to establish quite a novel way of getting him to disappear. One quiet Tuesday evening, they managed to persuade a local barmaid, Nicky, to lead him on in to one of the rundown pubs that he regularly frequented. At the end of her shift, she lured him in to the rear of the car park to a dark corner where the drunken old brute presumed that he was going to get lucky. Only he didn't realise that Darren and Luke would be lying in wait for him. As Nicky leaned forward to coax him towards her, Darren leapt into action and grabbed the shocked man, pulling him into the dimly lit disused alleyway next to the decrepit pub car park. Luke stepped out from the darkness and began punching him without mercy. Before the pissed old man had any idea what was happening he was knocked to the ground.

As the coward lay there begging for the beating to stop, Darren ushered Nicky away, gave her fifty pounds then told her to disappear. She never liked the slimy old bastard and his wandering hands, so she was only too pleased to help them set him up and earn fifty quid to boot. Spot on, she thought as she walked over to her red Fiesta, without even bothering to look back. Luke suddenly stopped battering him. Although he hated him for the way he had tortured and abused them over the years, for the first time in his life he felt pity for this miserable excuse of a man. He rolled him over so that through his bruised and swollen eyes he could see that it was his eldest son that had been handing out what he so regularly had done to the three of them. Luke simply said to him . 'Never come home again.' His father, tears in his eyes and coughing up blood, muttered, 'You won't see me again.' Then he rolled himself into a ball and began sobbing.

Uncle Darren came across, put his arm around Luke and slowly pulled him away. Luke shed a tear; after all, this shell of a man on the floor was still his father. The problem with a slimy rat bag like that is you never know when he will come crawling back from under whatever rock he has been hiding. At any rate, he would be gone for now.

Julie now had the freedom to begin working in Darren's shop on a weekend, and for once there was plenty of money in the Crooks' household without the harrying brute of a so-called father around taking and spending every penny that he could steal from them. Everything seemed to be running smoothly. Luke would take care of Mickey on a weekend. Being mildly autistic, Mickey could be difficult to deal with sometimes, but having said that, Luke found that with lots of cash in his pocket it was never too hard to keep him entertained. Going to the amusement arcade, to the swimming pool, down to Loftus Road to watch his beloved Queens Park Rangers and having a couple of cold lagers down at O'Neil's in Shepherd's Bush Green after the match was enough for Mickey Crooks to think he had the best life of any young man in West London. Mickey Crooks was a smashing kid; he always remained cheerful. His mother Julie would do anything for him, as she would Luke. The three of them were a lovely family, with a lot of love in their household.

Old Mr Kravis, who lived across the road, was good friends with Julie's mother and father. They had both passed away ten years ago, within six months of each other. They said that when her father died of bowel cancer, her mother missed her husband so much and she just could not bear to be without him; she simply gave up and died of a broken heart a few months later. This had upset Julie terribly – they were a small but tight-knit family and she felt let down by her mother, as she needed her mum's support more than ever when her dad died. Julie felt that cancer had robbed her of both parents, and she chose to wallow in self pity. She couldn't help feeling this way, she was just very bitter at how cruel life can be in such a short space of time. Luke, on the other hand, although saddened by the loss of his grandparents, stayed strong. In an odd way, all the beatings his father had given him since he was small had toughened him up. Although he did not realise it at the time, the support he gave his mother and younger brother, though Luke was only a boy himself, was nothing short of fantastic. He pulled his mum through what you could only describe as the closest thing you could get to a nervous breakdown. He got her up in the morning and helped her cope with Mickey's demands and needs. Feeding them both, Luke ran the show while still managing to get to school. All of this would only strengthen Luke's resolve for later in life. It had been a tough childhood: coping with a violent father, helping his mother through her near breakdown, looking after an autistic younger brother – if he could cope with all of this, anything could be possible. That was why the care and attention of his Uncle Darren was such a godsend while he was growing up; working with him in his shop seemed a world away from everyday life. Most importantly of all, it had given Luke the opportunity to make many good contacts with all sorts of, let us say, 'interesting' people.

One of the new interesting people Luke had come to know was a well-known 'character' – Danny Chilton, a man everyone tried to stay clear of. He was a proper villain; if anything illegal or not quite above board was going down, he would want to be involved in it. This would not be good news for Luke and Monks' future. Danny Chilton was unpredictable and his reputation went before him. Because he was five years older than the pair, Luke and Monks were not yet in the same league as Danny and his dodgy associates. However, Danny knew Uncle Darren reasonably well, and when he met Luke it did not take him long to work out that Luke was no mug. This boy has got a little bit about him, he thought. Danny had been keeping tabs on Luke and his mate for a while because he had an inkling that they were onto a nice little earner. Monks had been telling Luke for a couple of weeks now that he was positive that a connection of Danny Chilton's was asking about them, and on the drive back from Maidenhead the topic had come up once again.

'But why would he be interested in us?' asked Luke.

'I think that he wants in on the mobile phone scam,' Monks explained.

'No, you must have misheard.'

'Maybe so,' Monks conceded, 'but your uncle knows him.'

'And so what does that mean?'

'It means keep your ear to the ground.'

'Yeah, fair enough – we don't need that loony getting to know too much about us.'

'Exactly mate, so listen carefully,' said Monks as he pulled up in the BMW outside Uncle Darren's shop. Luke planned to ask his uncle for some background on Danny Chilton and his mob – he needed to find out if all the tales of murder and mayhem were true. He had heard so many rumours that it sometimes made Danny and his brother Jack sound like a modern-day version of the Kray twins.

3

A Fresh Start

Sydney

It was Saturday evening and Luke was showing his mate Monks the sights and sounds of Sydney. They were heading for The Hero of Waterloo, a picturesque old hotel, stopping at the many hostelries of The Rocks along the way. As they walked, Luke was explaining to Monks that the route they were taking was the Bradfield Highway, the road that leads down to The Rocks and Circular Quay, which is often referred to as the 'birthplace of Australia'. He tried impressing his old pal with some of the local knowledge that he had acquired since living there.

'It was here that the first human freight of convicts landed in January 1788,' he explained to him.

Monks could not have looked less interested. 'Oh yeah, really. How much further have we got to walk?' was his response. Why do I bother? thought Luke. 'We are nearly there,' he said. He realised that when they were supping in The Hero of Waterloo there would be no point in informing Monks that beneath their feet lay a tunnel once regularly used for smuggling, or that those sea captains who frequented the hotel were said to recruit patrons who drank too much by pushing them through trapdoors into the cellars and then leading them to the waiting ships through the same tunnel.

Why even try? Luke thought, remembering what an ignorant bastard he was at school. No fucking idea that boy, he told himself.

Luke had come out feeling healthy and happy, ready for a good night out. He always liked to start any evening out in the old part of Sydney anyway, so Monks would just have to put up with wherever Luke decided to take him. They were moving between specific types of historic hotels such as the Lord Nelson at Millers Point, which apparently was 'the oldest pub in Sydney' – or so the proprietor loved to let all the Japanese and American tourists know. They would believe just about anything you had to say, as long as your accent sounded authentic enough, which never failed to amuse Luke as the proprietor came from Manchester originally, and even though he had lived here for over fifteen years he had the worst mock Australian accent you've ever heard. Yet all the tourists lapped it up. Why not, they love it. Monks was looking distinctly unimpressed with the Lord Nelson. 'Are we near this pub you keep harping on about?' he asked.

'Yes mate, we'll go there after this drink.'

'Good, I don't think too much of this place to be honest, Luke,' Monks grumbled.

'Fair enough, let's move on.' They both lifted their glasses at the same time and swallowed the amber nectar.

Since meeting back up with Monks, Luke felt it was only right to try to keep his friend entertained, though he would like to know why he had turned up unexpectedly and not yet mentioned anything of home. So far, all Monks seemed to want to do was get pissed. All he had told Luke was that he had matured and changed his ways, promising Luke it wouldn't be like the old days. He was clean, he explained – he hadn't touched any gear for over six months. Of course, Luke believed him. Being a trusting chap he always remembered their oath and had given him the benefit of the

13

doubt. Anyway, it was great to catch up with an important person from his old life and to reminisce about days gone by. So Luke decided not to ask any awkward questions for now, although he did notice an old familiar look in Monks' eyes. One he remembered very well.

They finally arrived at The Hero of Waterloo, not a moment too soon as far as Monks was concerned. It was a favourite haunt of Luke's and he persuaded Monks to have a couple of drinks in there before heading into the city for maybe just an hour or two, both of them probably knowing full well that their good intentions of an early night after three beers or so would soon be forgotten. All of Luke's best-made plans of hopping onto a ferry at a reasonable time to be home on Manly Beach by ten o'clock, back to Shannon, beautiful, sexy Shannon, were about to be scuppered. Once these two started to sink a few bevvies, time became irrelevant.

Marc Crompton wasn't sure why or how he received the nickname 'Monks', but he thought it was quite a cool one, so he never bothered finding out. It was one of those things nobody knew. He stood at an imposing 6 feet 5 inches in height, with shoulder-length black curly hair pushed back behind his ears, a muscular well-toned body and thick neck muscles. Both his huge arms were tattooed in the style of sleeves – there was no room left on them to add any more. What really set him apart from your average hard-looking bastard were his eyes. He had cold, staring, evil eyes, the type you see in the newspapers associated with the most heinous of crimes. Murderers, rapists – these were Monks' eyes. He had a badly pockmarked face from terrible teenage acne, of which he was very conscious, always paranoid that people were mocking his bad skin. Mix all that up with a hostile attitude and the image is complete: one short-tempered, nasty bastard. Monks never needed much provocation – any excuse would start him off. Engaging in gratuitous casual violence was how he got his kicks, something that over the years he had made his own special craft.

By now Luke was feeling relaxed, happily chatting to his pal. More drinks went down, one after another, and they were laughing and joking. Immediately to their right were two young loud drunk Australians who were aggravating everybody around them with their boorish behaviour. Monks kept catching the eye of one of them, who responded by talking to his mate and laughing as if he was taking the piss out of him. Trying to pay no attention to the drunken loudmouth, Monks watched the plasma screen on the wall that was showing an Australian Rules football match rerun, as he did not want to upset Luke by causing a row. The trouble was he could only ignore the loudmouth for so long, as he had really begun to get under his skin.

'That bloke over there is starting to give me the hump,' Monks muttered to Luke.

'What bloke?'

'That prick over there keeps on staring at me.'

Luke turned to glance over his shoulder 'No he's not, don't take any notice.'

'Yeah, you're probably right.'

Luke had seen the warning signs. Monks had now decided that he required a little entertainment. Waiting for a chance to confront the noisy young Australian, he watched as the two of them intimidated people at will. He coerced Luke into moving slightly closer to his intended target without Luke realising that Monks was lining up the boisterous Australian and his pal for a good hiding. Knocking back his drink, Luke beckoned to his pal.

'Come on then, let's make our way into the city,' he said.

'Okay, I'll finish my beer,' said Monks, lifting the glass up in his huge hands then pouring the remnants down his throat. Out of the corner of his eye he spotted the loudmouth stumbling his way nearer into their course.

15

Monks held back for a second, then with a subtle action stepped back into the loudmouth's path. 'Sorry mate,' said the noisy Australian as he accidently bumped into Monks. 'No worries,' he replied calmly. The Australian muttered incoherently under his breath as he made his way to the toilet. Monks couldn't quite make out what the noisy Australian had said but he had convinced himself that it was derogatory or about his appearance. Taking a deep breath, he sighed and waited for the noisy Australian to return to the vicinity to see if he wished to repeat what he'd said.

By this point Luke had realised what was going on and was watching Monks' behaviour vigilantly.

'Easy now,' he said in a threatening tone as the noisy Australian returned from the toilet to make his way back to the bar. The young man looked up at Monks' fearsome appearance. Monks moved in close to the young man's face, with a stare that sent the shivers down his spine. He moved to one side and mumbled a nervous, 'Sorry, mate.' Deciding that he may need to keep out of this man's way, he scuttled back to his mate sharpish, not daring to look back. Monks sucked his teeth as he watched the young man move away.

Luke stepped in front of Monks. 'Leave it, mate, the kid doesn't want to know.'

'He needs to learn some fucking manners,' replied Monks.

'Not tonight, he isn't going to bother you – just let it go,' Luke said.

Monks stared with his fearsome eyes at Luke, then started laughing. 'You're right; it looks like he's shit himself.'

Much to Luke's relief the young Australian had decided to leave his drink and shoot out of the bar with his mate.

'Come on, it's your shout – get me a beer,' said Monks cheerily, pleased that he had scared the shit out of a young brash Australian. Luke, also happy that the two young men had left, went up to the bar to order two more Victoria Bitters, hoping that Monks would chill out for the rest of the night. He felt relieved that they could just have a couple more beers without having to worry about what that fucking lunatic was going to do.

One way of keeping lunatics under control is the opposite sex. If there was one thing Monks liked more than smashing people to a pulp, it was shagging women. As Luke returned with the schooners he was greeted with the sight of two attractive girls giggling away at Monk's witty repartee. Straight away, Luke's doubts got the better of him. They seemed familiar.

'Hey Luke, where the fuck have you been? Did you go and brew the stuff yourself?' said Monks, in a jocular mood.

'Did I take that long?' asked Luke.

'We nearly had to send out a search party – we thought you'd got lost, didn't we girls?' said Monks, at which both the girls giggled as he placed his arms around their waists and gave Luke a knowing wink. Fuck me; thought Luke, five minutes ago he wanted to kill some loudmouth Australian, now he is a comedian cracking the shittiest one-liners since the seventies.

'How you doing, ladies?' asked Luke, even though he had no real interest in chatting to the two girls. 'Good, thanks,' they replied concurrently. Monks pushed his head to the right to indicate his preferred choice of partner. What a cheeky bastard, thought Luke, he knows I would not cheat on Shannon so why is he tipping me the wink? Still, I might as well play along for a bit to keep myself amused. What harm can it do? He asked himself.

One of the girls was slightly built, with surfer-style bleached blonde hair and blue eyes – your stereotypical Australian. Her friend was almost identical, although Luke noticed she was a little larger in the chest, with green eyes. Clearly, the bigger chest had taken Monks' fancy.

17

'Over by the door there's a spare table,' said Green Eyes. 'Okay, let's take a seat,' responded the boys. So they moved across the floor to the table. The girls sat close to the window, pushing Luke and Monks into a corner, which set alarm bells ringing in Luke's head. Do not let your guard down, Luke thought as he took his seat and smiled at the girls. Monks, on the other hand, did not have a care in the world.

'I'm Leonie and she's Chloe,' said Green Eyes.

'Well, that's my pal Luke,' Monks said.

Luke sensed that the girls seemed uneasy as he smiled and said, 'Hello.'

'So what do you two Poms think of Oz then?' asked Leonie.

Luke took it on himself to answer for both of them. 'It's great, we're really enjoying ourselves so far,' he said.

'You bet we are, can't get enough of it,' said Monks, by now transfixed by Leonie's ample bosom. Luke adjusted his position so that he had a better view of the door. He studied Chloe, noticing that she kept looking at the side entrance of the pub.

'Are you girls local?' he asked.

'We're from Mosman, the North Shore – do you know it?' Chloe replied.

Luke loved the North Shore He had his heart set on eventually settling down there on Balmoral Beach, a quiet little enclave not too far from Mosman, once he had raised enough cash.

'Yeah, I know it. I bet it costs a few quid to live over there, though,' Luke said.

'Oh, I still live with my parents,' she answered.

'How old are you then, Chloe?'

'I will be nineteen next week.'

Not that Luke was interested – he only had eyes for Shannon. Still, she is a fit piece, he thought. With that, Leonie turned to Chloe and whispered in her ear.

'We'll not be a minute, boys, we're just going to the little girls' room,' she said, giggling as they stood up.

Luke waited until they had gone then said to Monks, 'There's a problem on its way, mate, I can feel it in my water.'

'Don't be soft, Luke, they're just a couple of tarts out for a good time,' Monks said, dismissively.

'Seriously, mate, they look familiar – I don't trust them,' Luke persisted.

'Listen, mate,' Monks said, 'I have not had a leg-over since Thailand, and I get the impression that big tits hasn't had a good seeing to for a while –' Luke interrupted. 'Mate, they look edgy,' he said, 'they're always looking around.'

'Don't be a twat, Luke.'

Not taking very long at all, the girls returned and squeezed round the table.

'Did you miss us, boys?' said Leonie. Luke smiled then decided not to answer.

'Of course we did, darling. Let's get some drinks in – come on, Luke, get to the bar, mate,' prompted Monks.

'Okay. What would you like'? Luke tried to chill out, even though it still didn't feel right.

As the night moved on, Monks was getting on very well with Green Eyes. They began to flirt with one another, then Monks' hands started to roam. The more his hands roamed the closer they became. Luke tried to keep a polite conversation going with Chloe, all the usual small talk, while his pal seemed to be edging closer towards what he desired. Luke could not help but feel apprehensive as he watched Monks and Leonie cautiously, who by now were engaged in a world of their own. Chloe, he noticed, was continuously checking her mobile phone. She was nervously sitting on her hands and did not look comfortable chatting to Luke at all. Then suddenly it clicked into place – the pair were only there to set them up. He recalled seeing them at the bar with the two drunk Australians. Only a matter of time now, Luke thought.

'Monks, can I have a word?' said Luke.

'Yeah, what's the matter?' he replied.

Luke nodded over to an unused fireplace and they walked across to the mantelpiece. 'Remember the two loudmouths earlier on? Well, I've just realised that I saw Leonie and Chloe with them.'

'Are you sure?'

'Positive,' replied Luke.

'Fuck it,' said Monks. 'I really wanted to shaft her tonight – now I want to hurt her.'

Both of them now realised that time was of the essence. Luke was even more annoyed than Monks – they had fallen for one of the oldest tricks in the book.

'Right, how long do you think they've kept us here?' Monks asked.

'About an hour and a half, I reckon,' Luke guessed.

'Well, they're probably here with back-up.'

Casting a menacing look in the girls' direction, Monks gave the game away. Green Eyes sussed immediately, took out her mobile and frenetically began to dial. Monks pointed at them both as they got up and made for the exit. The place was packed to the rafters, with a good Saturday night buzz about it. Luke looked around for the quickest escape route, knowing that the two loudmouths with their little back-up team would soon be arriving. In fact, they were already there. As the girls fled, Luke and Monks both realised that an attack was imminent.

Monks was now in his element. Those two tarts can wait, he thought. Luke, on the other hand, was still scanning the area for all possible options. Anyone could be a potential attacker by this point. Leonie and Chloe had probably identified Luke and Monks and the two loudmouths were most likely outside waiting for the fun to begin. Needing to be extra vigilant, they began to work together, just like old times. Luke's worst fears were confirmed as they were now in danger, and he was beginning to feel like he used to. It was something he had always worked so hard to prevent. Monks turned to a couple of young noisy aggressive Australians to the left of him, trying to read their demeanour. His radar told him that these two were not involved – they were too interested in watching the barmaid bending over to pick up a crate of empty bottles. Even though they seemed lively, they were just not twitchy enough to be spoiling for a fight. Luke stayed on the right-hand side of Monks, now very aware and completely focused on anybody that looked to be coming towards them. The door on the right was slightly ajar, and through it he spotted Green Eyes indicating to a heavily built, bordering on fat, older man where he and Monks were inside. First mistake, he thought – we now know one of the loudmouth's entourage, we just need to see how many more of them there are.

'Here they come, Monks, a big fat man will be leading them in from the right,' said Luke.

'Got you mate, I'm ready,' Monks replied.

A tall lean wiry chap with an odd look etched on his face came in, followed by the large bloke. The loudmouth and his crony tried to remain out of view, hanging around outside with Green Eyes and Chloe by the door. Weighing up the opposition, Monks searched around for potential weapons. He was psyched-up and ready for action. The heavily built man and the tall chap made their way towards them. Luke and Monks pretended not to see them coming. Always let your enemy think that they have the upper hand – that was how they used to do it. By letting the enemy feel that they were not expecting an attack they would keep the element of surprise, then all of a sudden let them have it. The heavily built man headed for the bar and tried to barge Monks out of the way, getting no reaction from him. Monks took a step back. The tall lean wiry chap turned to stare down Luke, who responded by putting up his hand as if to apologise.

The heavily built man, sensing that Monks was backing off, barged into him once more – still no reaction from him. The tall lean wiry chap turned back towards the heavy man and said, 'These two are a couple of faggots.' Nodding in agreement the heavily built man laughed and said, 'You get these Poms coming over here, thinking they own the place. But they're usually full of shit.' As they continued to take the piss out of Luke and Monks, the loudmouth and his crony re-entered the hotel. Monks grabbed an empty glass from a nearby table, hiding it behind his back. The loudmouth, by now feeling anxious, tried to keep out of sight, while watching the situation with his crony. They moved sheepishly through the crowd, trying to sneak up behind Luke and Monks inch by inch, as if stalking their prey.

Unknown to them, Luke was monitoring them out of the corner of his eye every step of the way. He gave Monks a knock to signal it was now or never. Their two adversaries again faced Luke and Monks, full of hostility. 'You cannot come in here and bully our mate, you Pom –' the heavily built man did not get the opportunity to finish his sentence. A small crowd of thirtysomethings, out for a quiet drink, stood open-mouthed as the violence flared right in front of them. Before another word was uttered, Monks swapped the glass from his left hand to his right behind his back, brought it around his waist in one swift uppercut movement at a slight angle and smashed the glass into the unsuspecting man's face, catching him bang on top of his left eye. The glass shattered with a sickening crack and Monks pulled the broken glass downwards sharply to lacerate the guy's face from his eye to the top of his mouth. As the poor victim fell to the ground, Monks threw the glass at the optics behind the bar.

As soon as the glass connected, Luke had jumped into action, punching the tall lean wiry chap square in the bollocks. Luke stood watching as the air was sucked out of the man's lungs. He doubled over in pain, desperately trying to catch his breath. The loudmouth and his crony were now only a yard or so from Luke and Monks. Luke faced them to see that they had not come any closer. Monks was now viciously stamping on the heavily built man's head, as he lay unconscious. The loudmouth and his crony seemed to be having second thoughts after witnessing their friends being dispatched with such ease.

The tall lean wiry chap was still wriggling around on the deck gasping for air. He had started to irritate them both. Monks had become restless while waiting for his unconscious heavily built friend to stir and decided to try to send tall lean wiry chap to sleep. He picked up an empty glass from the bar, aimed at the tall chap's head and brought his right arm over his shoulder in an action as if he were bowling a bouncer in an Ashes test match. He released the glass from his hand, aiming directly for the wiry chap's skull. Fortunately for his target, Monks' radar was a little off. Instead of cutting his face to ribbons, the glass hit him in the ribcage with terrific force, bounced off in one piece over his head then shattered by Luke's feet. He was already struggling to breathe with the wind knocked out of him and had a pair of aching bollocks – a broken rib to boot certainly did not make the tall guy's evening any more pleasant. The loudmouth and his crony were now frozen to the spot with fear as Monks twisted in their direction, pointed at them and stared, his eyes full of evil intent. The colour drained rapidly from their faces and they made a hasty departure, abandoning their injured pals. Several of the patrons had by now left the bar, sickened at what they had seen. The thirtysomething crowd had moved as far away as possible.

A surreal moment of calm now ensued as silence descended upon the hotel. In what seemed like an eternity, Luke assessed the circumstances, thinking fast, and figured out that it was time to leave. Looking at Monks he said, 'Time to go.'

'He hasn't had enough yet,' Monks replied.

Luke started to panic. He knew it would not be long before the police arrived, so they had to shift in the next few minutes. He did not need to get arrested tonight or indeed any night at all. He cursed himself and his own stupidity – why had he let Monks back in to his life? He would always cause problems for him. No worries for nearly six months, now it's all gone tits up, he thought. As Luke surveyed the state of play once more, he took into account how badly the two on the floor were injured. A large space had opened up around them, that strange silence still lingering over the place. Monks breathed deeply. The crowd stayed back, obviously concerned for the two men hurt, but nobody was prepared to step forward to help.

Eventually, the heavily built man began to come round. Luke tried to distract Monks as his body started to twitch. Grabbing his pal by the arm he led him to the door, the crowd parting in front of them. Just as they were ready to exit, the prone man let out a loud moan as the pain surging through his head brought him around. 'My face! My face!' he cried. Hearing this, Monks was annoyed – the man had woken up, and now he had to decide whether to administer more punishment or not.

Turning back to the bar, he was pleased with all the extra space that had been created by the still shocked patrons of the hotel. Monks manoeuvred himself into a position to inflict as much damage as possible. People were standing by, trying not to get involved, watching the man crying hysterically and writhing from side to side in agony. He was trying to hold his face together, but it was hopeless. Blood kept on pouring through his hands with no indication of stopping any time soon. Luke could do no more. Monks now had the smell of blood in his nostrils. He was going back in for the kill.

The tall chap scrambled to his feet and scuttled away to try to take sanctuary in the toilets, hoping he would escape any more violence. Luke watched him all the way, a look of absolute terror etched onto his face as he disappeared. Monks was taking his time to weigh up all the angles, still deciding whether to leave his opponent or wound him some more. He is such a sick bastard, thought Luke as he watched his friend enjoying the moment, the heavily built man lying there with his face hanging off and wincing like a beaten dog. His mind now made up, Monks waited a touch longer, allowing his victim to make out that he was still there. The man looked up at him and saw what was coming. Monks shouted at him: 'You've not had enough yet.' And then he started running the short distance towards him, drawing back his preferred right leg so he would be able to kick the man as hard as he possibly could. Monks managed to put all of his nearly 16 stone of bulk behind the most brutal of kicks perfectly placed onto the jaw of the already beaten and badly cut man. There was a loud thud as the right foot connected. Instantly, the defenceless man stopped making any noise.

Luke grimaced as he stood watching, praying that this would satisfy Monks' bloodlust. Monks stopped and admired his work; the heavily built man's head was smashed to a pulp, the skin from his left eye to the top of his mouth flapped over to expose his gums and teeth, and blood was starting to congeal over fragments of glass stuck in and around the ugly wound. Monks couldn't resist one final humiliation – he stamped on his groin with as much force as he could muster, but his victim was by now completely unconscious, and his broken body made no movement at all.

4

Meeting the Girl

England

It was Friday night and Luke and Monks were planning a night out with their mates. The bright lights of the city were always beguiling for a group of young single men on a weekend, especially in London, one of the most exciting cities in the world. They liked to get up to the West End a couple of times a month. Luke had promised his Uncle Darren that he would open the shop at six the next morning, but he decided that he would go out with the lads anyway – he'd just have to make sure that he was home reasonably early.

'Go on Luke, I'll close the shop,' said his Uncle Darren, generously. 'Have a good night – but remember, you're opening for me tomorrow.'

'Cheers Darren, I won't forget.' Result, thought Luke as he grabbed his coat then left the shop to go home and get ready. Outside the shop, Luke passed Danny Chilton.

'Is your uncle in there, son?' he asked Luke.

'Yes mate, he is,' Luke replied. Do not call me son, Luke thought as he walked past him.

Luke was curious why Danny kept on going into his uncle's shop, as he had never seen him buy anything. He decided to wait around to see if anything looked suspicious and returned to the shop window. He stood slightly out of the eye line of his uncle and Danny and watched as they shook hands then shared a joke. Satisfied that nothing looked threatening or out of the ordinary, Luke presumed that they were almost certainly old pals, and turned around and made tracks for home.

Inside the shop, the conversation was heading towards Luke's budding business acumen.

'I hear your nephew and his sidekick are making waves in the mobile phone industry,' Danny stated.

Realising that Danny was making enquiries that might not benefit Luke in the near future, Darren tried to play down his nephew's successful enterprise, saying, 'They are only pulling a pound here and there, Danny.'

'Well, that's not what I'm being told.'

Darren paused slightly before he replied. 'Who is telling you that? I don't think –'

'Don't take me for a mug, Darren, I want to be involved,' said Danny abruptly, interrupting him.

'I understand – I'll have a word with the kid,' Darren said quietly.

Danny smiled at this, then calmly informed Darren, 'That's all I'm asking for – just a little involvement, then everybody's happy.'

Danny put out his hand. Darren reluctantly shook hands with him.

'I'll call back in sometime next week to sort out the fees with your boy.'

Danny then picked up a can of lemonade from the fridge, calling out to Darren, 'See you soon.' He did not bother to pay for it and walked out of the shop.

Darren sighed. He had hoped that his nephew would not have to deal with Danny Chilton and his nasty mob; unfortunately, this had now become unavoidable. He decided that he would talk to Luke about it the next day and give him some sound advice on what he would need to do to keep Danny off his case.

Arriving home, Luke walked in to find Mickey sat in the lounge watching television. Mr Kravis was standing in the kitchen chatting to his mum and as always he was making her laugh out loud with his daft jokes. Good old Mr Kravis, thought Luke, I wonder where his granddaughter is? She had left to go backpacking around Europe, but she had been gone for a good while now.

'Hello, Luke, how are you young man?' a cheerful Mr Kravis asked.

'I'm fine, thank you,' said Luke as he passed him and kissed his mother.

'Hello darling, do you want a cup of tea?'

'No thanks, mum, I'm going to take a shower, then I'm off out for the night.'

'Okay, love.'

Luke smiled at Mr Kravis then went upstairs to change and freshen up.

'All right, donut,' he yelled to Mickey as he passed the living room.

'Yes, dickhead!' the lad retorted. They both laughed as Luke bounded up the stairs.

It was a different scene altogether at Monks' house. He never really spoke to his siblings – they were all a fair bit older than he was and had left home – and his parents were by now quite elderly. It was as if he did not fit. Perhaps this could explain some of his strange behaviour from time to time. His two older brothers never took any notice of him at all when he was growing up. They would often come around to visit their parents on a Friday, and this evening, as usual, they acknowledged Monks with only a nod of the head in his direction, to which he responded in kind. That was it –

nothing more to say. Not that he cared, as he had always thought since a young age that those two brothers of his were a couple of pricks.

He did have an affinity with his sister – she at least showed him some attention when he was small. Apart from all that, Monks had always felt that his parents did not really want him. He must have been an accident, conceived later on in life at a moment of drunken celebration, after a wedding or some other auspicious occasion. This, however, could not be further from the truth; he may not have had a very close bond with his brothers, or his sister, but his parents loved him just as much as the other three. It was just that they were too old to become parents again when Marc Crompton was born. It was unfortunate that by the time Monks started school all his siblings had left home, so he never had the chance to get to know them. This was not through lack of trying – he just came along too late.

For a young West London boy, getting ready for a night on the town was all part of the fun. Luke was a snappy dresser and liked to take his time choosing what to wear for an evening out. Dress to impress was his motto – if you don't care what you look like, why should anybody else give a monkey's? And so he took a great deal of pride in his appearance. After getting out of the shower, the ritual would begin. Moving into his bedroom he would open the wardrobe to study the vast selection of clothes that were hanging in the closet. Everyone was in there – Dolce & Gabbana, Yves Saint Laurent, Armani, Hugo Boss and Stone Island, to name just a few, and of course you have to own all the British classics such as Ben Sherman, Fred Perry and Hackett. You name it, Luke had it all in there – the boy loved clothes. He also had every designer brand of shoe and trainer you could think of.

Studying this never-ending assortment of clobber, he

decided on a long-sleeved pink checked Henri Lloyd shirt, with a pair of Diesel straight-cut denims. To finish the ensemble he chose a light-brown pair of Ben Sherman Chelsea boots. He placed a silver thumb ring on his right hand, and then had to remove it to put a handful of re-mouldable putty in his hair to style it just the way he liked. Checking himself out in his full-length mirror, Luke was pleased with what he saw. He was ready to hit the West End with all of the chaps.

This was where he bumped into her. Having a beer up in Soho, it was Monks who spotted her first. Tall, brunette, bronzed and with a figure to die for, she certainly stood out from the crowd. He nudged Luke and said, 'I wouldn't mind giving her one, would you?'

Luke glanced across, catching her eye, and then responded, 'Too right, mate – she is well fit.' She was still looking in Luke's direction as he spoke. He could feel his face going red with embarrassment as she gestured to him as if to say, 'I can lip-read and I saw what you just said to your friend.' Luke turned away to continue his conversation with Monks.

'She's looking over here – I'm going to get in there,' said Monks.

'No chance mate, she looks too classy for you,' laughed Luke, thinking quietly to himself, leave it out mate – I fancy her.

'Maybe, but she will fall for the old Monks' charm,' he returned, then confidently strolled over towards her. Luke stood with his pals, watching intently.

'He's on the pull straight away then,' commented Jon, or Powerpack as they called him due to his short stature and the rapid left hook he possessed. It came in handy in times of need, often surprising a recipient who had tried to intimidate him and made the mistake of miscalculating his strength based on his size. The old adage of never judge a book by its cover could not be truer in Powerpack's case.

'You know Monks,' another of their drinking friends added. Luke laughed along, but inside he was hoping Monks would get the knock-back. Luke carried on chatting to his pals and Monks returned five minutes later, saying, 'Must be mad, that bird.' He sounded stunned as they all laughed at him, knowing he had failed to impress. 'Why's that mate, don't she like ugly men?' They all chuckled and began to take the piss out of him.

'You never guess what though, boys,' Monks said.

They still mocked him some more.

'Shut up lads,' said Luke. 'What did she tell you, Monks?'

'No, it doesn't matter.'

'Come on, Monks, don't be a dick.'

'Well, as I was giving her the chat she kept on asking who you were, Luke. I told you – she is clearly mental.'

Luke's heart was in his mouth – he was delighted.

'There you go, boys – a woman with good taste. I could tell she had a bit of class about her.'

All the lads jeered Luke as he grinned at them all.

'Better get a move on, son – that big black geezer is chatting her up now.'

Luke looked over at her to see she was talking to the dude, but she seemed to have her gaze firmly fixed in Luke's vicinity as if to say, 'Are you coming over to buy me a drink, or what?'

'Get in there, son,' piped up a couple of the lads in a good-humoured manner. She was still staring over. Monks did not like it one bit; although Luke was his best mate, he couldn't handle rejection very well. Outwardly, it seemed that he was laughing and cajoling Luke along with the rest of them, but inwardly he was fuming, already deciding that her refusal of his advances and the fact that the lads were taking the piss out of him would now mean that unless some tasty piece got the benefit of his carnal knowledge later in the evening, then some poor sap would be getting his head kicked in before the sun rose in the morning.

31

The big black dude looked unhappy – it seemed that he had just had the brush off from the fine-looking young woman, which encouraged Luke's pals to wind him up just a touch more. If I don't go over there now, this lot will be taking the piss all night, Luke thought. She looked at him again, so Luke finished his bottle of Beck's, placed it on the table, pushed back his shoulders and then, casual as you like, sauntered across the crowded bar to catcalls and taunts from his mates.

As he approached her, Luke felt his heart begin to race. He never usually worried about chatting up girls – being a rather confident chap he just did not think about it. Somehow this felt different, he did not know why.

'Took your time in coming over to see me, didn't you?' she said, in a prominent Australian accent.

Luke was stunned for a second by the confidence of this gorgeous Australian woman standing in front of him. 'Yeah, I saw my friend talking to you –' before he could say any more than that, she interrupted him.

'I did not like him at all – too full of himself.'

Luke laughed then started to relax. 'You're right; he can be a bit overbearing.'

'You're not wrong – what a big head. I reckon he thought he could do me in the ladies toilets .'

Luke loved her brashness. He couldn't remember meeting such a straight-talking girl before, and he had known a few confident London girls in his time.

'Are you going to buy me a drink, then?'

'What would you like, and what's your name?'

'Shannon. What's yours?'

'Luke.'

'Nice to meet you, Luke – I'll have a rum and coke, please.'

With that, Luke went off to the bar. He really liked the way Shannon held herself. The fact that Monks had been blown out by a smart, sexy, quick-firing, fine-looking girl was the icing on the cake. Monks hardly ever got the knock-back; even though he was an ugly bastard he always managed to pull. Perhaps he scared them into bed, who knows. Not this time, though – the fit girl fancied Luke. It did amuse him, and he raised his hand to the boys, who were watching what he was up to, chatting to the best-looking girl in the place. They all waved back at him – even Monks seemed to be in the spirit for a bit of light-hearted banter.

'So what brings an Australian girl to London, then?'

A bit of an obvious chat-up line, but at least it was a little more original than 'Do you come here often?', Luke thought.

'I've done a bit of modelling back home in Sydney, but nothing seemed to be happening so I thought I would try my luck in the old country,' Shannon replied.

'Oh, you are from here originally, then?'

'Well, I think my granddad was a Pom – Manchester, I was told.'

Luke took a sip of his lager. Shannon carried on talking.

'So you're a real life cockney then, are you?'

Luke nearly spat out his beer as he laughed.

'What's so funny – what have I said?' Shannon asked.

Luke tried hard to stop himself from giggling at her question. 'No, I'm not a cockney, I come from West London – that's the East End you're thinking of, they're the ones you see on the television.'

Shannon looked slightly embarrassed as Luke stopped laughing. Shit, thought Luke, I hope I haven't put her off. He need not have worried – Shannon fancied Luke, big style.

'How come you all talk the same?' she joked with him.

'Do we? I haven't noticed,' said Luke.

'Really? You don't think you do?'

Luke paused. 'I suppose when you grow up in a city like this, you can pick out the different accents of London easily.'

As they were chatting away they moved in closer to each

other; they had a connection, as if they had known each other all their lives. Somehow, this felt right for both of them – everything seemed to be going well. All too well. Just then, Powerpack arrived from the opposite side of the pub. 'Luke, mate, you'd better come and give us a hand – Monks is starting to kick off with a couple of Tottenham lads over at the bar.'

Oh no, Luke thought, not now, Monks, please – he knows that I'm well in here.

'What's wrong?' Shannon asked, concerned.

Luke said to her, 'I won't be a minute – my mate's in a bit of trouble. I'll be back soon.'

'Come on, you mugs,' Monks was shouting, now that he could see out of the corner of his eye that Luke had reappeared. The Tottenham lads did not seem even the slightest bit interested in Monks' challenge, as they did not have a clue why he had all of a sudden decided to try to start on them. They simply turned around and left the pub. Monks did not notice them leave, as he was focused on Luke coming across to help his friend.

'I knew you would back me up,' he said. Then he turned to face his targets, only to see that they had disappeared. 'Where did they go?' The relief on the boys' faces that Monks' targets had now gone was evident.

Although Monks thought the world of Luke, he certainly didn't like the fact that the fit Australian bird had rebuked him because she had obviously had her vision fixed on Luke from the very start of their brief conversation. This was the only reason that Monks tried to cause a fight in the pub, knowing that the kerfuffle would distract Luke and bring him to his aid. Monks was disappointed that the two lads had done a runner as he fancied a row; still, he had managed to ruin Luke's chances with the fit Australian girl, he thought to himself, looking back across the bar to see that she had gone.

Luke said to Monks, 'Can't you stay out of trouble for five minutes?'

To which he laughed and said, 'Well, they've cleared off now; you can go back to your bird,' thinking that she had left.

'I will. Try to behave yourself, mate – I may well be in here.'

Luke turned to return to the other side of the pub, and Monks' smile was instantly wiped off his face as he saw the fit Australian girl walking back to where she had been sitting to wait for Luke. He thought his performance had put her off Luke – it had not. Realising he had failed, Monks turned to Powerpack and said, 'Get the beers in.'

Luke went back to Shannon and apologised for shooting off to help Monks at the bar.

'That's okay,' she said, 'I've got a friend like that back home who can't seem to keep out of trouble.'

'He's a good lad really, but he can be a right pain in the arse sometimes,' Luke explained.

Shannon began laughing; she noticed that Monks was watching them with a look of resentment etched onto his face. She could tell immediately that he was jealous of Luke. She truly did not like him; she was a good judge of character and could tell that, no doubt about it, Luke's best mate Monks was bad news. Shannon moved in close to Luke, still with an eye on Monks. 'So when are you going to take me out for dinner?' she asked. Luke, though slightly taken aback by her marvellous self-confidence, was delighted that she seemed so keen.

'When are you next free, and where do you want to go?'

'Well, I'll leave that up to you. How about tomorrow night?'

Sorted, thought Luke. 'Tomorrow sounds good. Anyway, we still have tonight for a couple of drinks – what do you say, you up for it?'

Shannon had decided to ignore Monks, who was constantly staring over at them. 'I'll have another rum and coke,' she replied.

'No problem.' Grinning from ear to ear, Luke stood up and went over to the bar.

Later, Luke was still deep in conversation with Shannon when Monks came over. 'Come on mate, we're off to a club in about ten minutes.'

'All right, I'll meet you there later. Where are you lot going?' asked Luke.

'Go with your friends,' Shannon butted in. 'I have an interview for an assignment tomorrow, so I need to get home soon.'

Monks half sneered at her as he wandered back over to the rest of the boys.

'So what time shall we meet tomorrow night?' asked Luke.

'Well, the appointment I have is at four, so I can meet up with you at eight,' Shannon replied.

'What's the interview for?'

'It's a modelling shoot.'

'Easy then – how can they say no?' And then he gave her his killer smile.

'You are quite the charmer,' she said, fluttering her eyelashes at him. 'Now shoot off with your mates – they're waiting for you. We shall meet up tomorrow.'

'Yeah, I'm looking forward to it.'

'So you should be,' she joked, and then she kissed Luke on the cheek. 'See you.'

'Yeah, don't be late.' Shannon gave him a playful shove. Monks was still monitoring her; she gave him a little wink as Luke turned to meet his pals. Monks ignored her. All the lads cheered as Luke turned and waved at Shannon, then they all finished their drinks and left the pub. As they were walking out Monks said to Luke, 'Are you taking that slag out then?'

'Yes, don't be a cock, Monks – she's no slag.' Monks did not say another word.

Around the time that Luke and his pals were heading over to the club, a baby-blue Bentley pulled up in White City housing estate, where the large tenements blocked out the grey rain-filled sky. The thickset driver, George Rixon, stepped out of the car, followed almost immediately by another man nicknamed Pug, due to the fact that his nose was spread flat across his face like a boxer's. They opened the rear doors and Danny Chilton emerged from one side, his brother Jack from the other. Rixon went to the back of the car and opened the boot. All four of them stood at the rear of the car as the driver pulled out a large black holdall then shut the boot. Danny nodded to the driver and he reciprocated. They all looked at Danny then they proceeded to enter the estate.

As they trudged up to the fourth floor on dimly lit stairwells with graffiti-covered walls, they were careful to avoid stepping on the many discarded needles that lay on the ground with other drug paraphernalia. This piss-stained sink estate was not exactly the best place in London to be at any time of the day. Danny took a step back then gave the signal to his driver, his brother Jack standing next to him. Rixon knocked on the door; they waited about ten seconds – no answer. He knocked louder and harder this time. A shadow appeared in the hallway, and then went out of view; a moment later two shadows appeared and one slowly approached the front door. The scrawny figure neared the door then stepped back again. 'Who is it?'

Danny stood in front of his brother and driver. 'It's Danny. Now open the door, son.'

A silence followed. 'What do you want?'

'Don't piss around, son, let us in or we'll take the door off its hinges.'

More silence, until the scrawny figure came closer and opened the door to let them into the flat. Rixon entered first with Pug the co-driver right behind him, then Danny and Jack followed. 'Get in the front room with your pal; we want a quick word.' The scrawny figure walked in with them – his pal was already in there waiting.

'Do you know who I am?' is a phrase that can spark either laughter or fear. Unhappily for these two reprobates, it would be the latter. The scrawny character was 5 foot 8 inches tall and had the worn-out features of a long-term addict. He didn't have the foggiest who these people were, although his partner in crime, also a rather tired-looking heroin addict, regrettably did.

'I know who you are,' he said.

'Good, I won't bother to introduce myself,' said Danny. Scrawny was now confused – he was aware that they robbed and stole to feed their filthy habit, but who the fuck were these four heavy-looking men in his flat?

'Hang on a minute, I don't know who you are –' Before he could continue, Danny intervened.

'Your friend doesn't need any explanation, so I'll let him tell you,' he said, turning to his friend. 'Carry on, young man, please enlighten him.'

His partner swallowed hard and began to let his scrawny friend know. 'He's Danny Chilton, and that's his brother Jack; they run the manor.' Scrawny gazed into space, realising this mob were not here for a cosy chat.

'Right, now we have been introduced, I presume you know why we are here.'

The two addicts stared at one another. Neither of them could work out which one of them had upset Danny and his mob. They often stole and mugged victims together, never on their own, so they shrugged their shoulders and remained completely silent. Rixon dropped the large black holdall in front of them, bent down and unzipped the bag. As he did this, Danny moved to make himself some space and started to speak.

'You owe an associate of mine a fair bit of money.'

They looked at each other again. Jack and Pug moved towards one of the pair. Danny continued, 'A month or so ago, you two robbed a house in Ladbroke Grove. Is it coming back to you yet?'

The pair had robbed so many houses in the last couple of months; they honestly could not remember any specific house. They were off their heads on heroin after almost every burglary.

'Okay lads, let's get on with it,' Danny said, putting his right arm into the large black holdall and pulling out a small cosh. He began to tap it menacingly against his left hand. The scrawny addict started to panic as Rixon smashed his granite-like fist into his fellow addict's jaw, knocking him to the ground. Pug moved across and lifted him straight back up onto his feet. Dazed and confused, the addict's lips swelled up immediately. He was pinned upright against the living room wall by Pug as Rixon hit him in the exact same spot again. He went silent and looked completely out of it.

'Take what you want – there's a load of money under the floorboards over by the window,' Scrawny told them, almost in tears.

'Oh, did I not explain? My associate doesn't want his belongings returned.'

Jack reached into the holdall, rummaged around for a bit, then pulled out a pickaxe handle. Pug let the dead-eyed looking addict drop to the floor. He curled up into a ball to try to protect his head. 'Look – take all the money, it's yours. I'm sorry – please take it all.'

'Too late for that, we are not here for your money, we don't even want it.'

Scrawny realised he was in for a beating at the very least and started sobbing, hoping for mercy. Jack casually walked over to dead eyes, who lay perfectly still. Standing over him, he proceeded to smash the pickaxe handle onto his skull three times in a fast pump action. Blood began pouring from the poor fellow's cranium. He remained perfectly still and did not make a sound.

Jack took a breather, and then began wiping the blood off the pickaxe handle onto the shabby, stained curtain that was hanging by the window. Danny was now directly in front of the sobbing scrawny . He decided to hold fire for a wee bit longer, as he wanted to watch the Scrawny one break down. Danny smiled as he noticed the front of Scrawny's pale Adidas tracksuit bottoms darken in the groin area as he wet himself with fear. Rixon looked away in disgust at this sorry sight; he hoped Danny would just get on with it. He may well have performed violent acts on the orders of his boss, but nevertheless he certainly was not comfortable watching a weasel of a man humiliate himself. This was the complete opposite of Danny and Jack – they were almost getting off on watching this desperate Scrawny, who was now on his knees, begging for mercy. Pug felt the same way as Rixon; to take their minds off this pathetic scene they went to pick the motionless man up off the floor. As they moved him, it became clear that the man was dead, so they dropped him back to the floor. 'Danny, he's gone,' Rixon said. To which his boss replied, 'Oh dear – looks as if we'll have to do this one as well.' Scrawny, whose bowels had now emptied almost completely, seemed to accept his fate; he looked at his dead friend lying unmoving in the corner of the room. Danny was composed and was ready to beat this weak and desperate drug addict to death, and was looking forward to doing so.

And yet, in seeing his friend murdered, Scrawny found an inner strength. Although he had been begging for his life, had pissed and shit himself several times, he suddenly decided that he would determine his own fate. When Danny and Jack were only inches away from him, he rose to his feet, stopped sobbing and looked Danny between the eyes. 'Fuck you, Chilton.'

'No, boy – you're the one that's fucked.' Danny grinned at him then raised his cosh in readiness to start battering the man to a pulp. The scrawny and – up to this point – gutless addict smiled at them both, then, in a sharp movement, turned and at full pelt ran the four short steps to the thin

40

pane of glass that passed as a window of the fourth-floor flat, and threw his skinny body straight through it. As the glass came out of the frame and the addict disappeared, Danny stood there, shocked. They all stood still looking at each other.

'Well, fuck me, I didn't expect that,' he exclaimed. Then he began to laugh, and in turn they all did. 'Where did he say they have some cash?'

'Under the floorboards, by the window,' said Rixon. He pulled up the boards and found a couple of grand.

'Right, let's fuck off before the Old Bill turn up.'

Danny kicked the man in the corner to make sure he was dead; he was. They could already hear police sirens. One after the other they left the flat; none of them said a word as they walked back to the car. Nobody even bothered to look out of their window to see a dead man on the concrete four storeys below.

5

Getting Across the Harbour

Sydney

Shannon Rodman climbed out of the shower, grabbing hold of a large white towel. She dried her short brunette hair then rubbed her eyes. Taking hold of a separate towel, she began to swab down the mirror, the wet room now resembling a sauna. Having her shower so hot meant that visibility became virtually impossible. Once she had wiped a large section of the full-length mirror and the steam began to clear, Shannon could see her reflection, her skin pink from the red-hot water she liked to stand under. She never felt truly refreshed unless she could feel the burn of hot water.

Next, she took some moisturising cream and massaged the cooling essence into her high cheek bones, her big brown eyes looking back at her. Finishing her face massage routine, she plucked her eyebrows, and then prepared for the next stage of her compulsive beauty ritual, which would take her more than an hour to complete. The full-length mirror was now completely steam free and Shannon could see her whole body. She stretched across the double vanity and reached for her preferred body lotion. There was only a small amount left; holding it upside down she just about managed to squeeze out a handful to gently rub together.

She always started in precisely the same way. First, she

massaged from her neck down onto her shoulders, in a slow circular motion. Then, she gradually moved down over her ample firm breasts, onto her flat, petite stomach. Turning to the right, she smoothed over her gorgeous long legs that led up to her optimum feature. Oh yes, no doubt about it whatsoever – she had to agree with the many admirers that commented as she would pass by that it was one fine-looking ass. Not surprisingly, she had done a little modelling from time to time. At only twenty-four years old she could do a little more, she thought, as the last of the moisturiser absorbed into her smooth skin. Remembering the last modelling gig she had done a few short months ago in London, in a seedy dank room somewhere off Wardour Street in Soho, she shuddered and pushed the unpleasant memory from her mind.

Putting on a clean, crisp, comfortable robe, she moved into the hallway, through to the spacious living room of her large penthouse apartment. She felt safe here, at home. Now relaxed and at ease with the world, Shannon picked up a cigarette and waited until she got onto her balcony before lighting it. Sitting on one of the chaise longues furthest away from the sliding doors, she took a long, slow drag from the menthol cigarette, enjoying the icy sensation as the smoke hit the back of her lungs, then blew the smoke out into the air. Although she enjoyed the occasional cigarette, Shannon never smoked inside her apartment – she utterly despised the stale smell of tobacco. She often wondered why she smoked at all, as after every cigarette she would spray on her Gucci eau de perfume, and then suck on a packet of extra-strong mints, paranoid that anybody would be able to smell the smoke on her. It was a strange quirk, she knew, but Shannon just couldn't stand the idea of people thinking that she smoked.

Standing up to extinguish the cigarette in a small ashtray that she always kept at the furthest end of the balcony from the apartment, she leaned over the railing, enjoying the revitalising early evening air as it was beginning to cool down. She watched the towering Norfolk pines as they gently swayed in rhythm with the waves lapping on the shore. The sun had now begun to set on Manly Beach at the end of a hot Saturday and the day-trippers and tourists were making their way off the beach onto the promenade towards Manly Wharf to head back to the city. Taking all of this in, Shannon settled back onto the chaise longue, which was positioned high enough up that she could watch them all wander by without anyone being able to see her. Closing her eyes she caught the last of the sun before it finally disappeared under the horizon. She decided to rest there for a while, to put her feet up for half an hour or so. Feeling good, she took a few moments to survey her surroundings. The apartment was spacious and pristine; the three other chaises longues spread across the balcony lay empty for now. She had come a long way to own all of this, and through her own endeavour. It was all so easy – an old friend of hers, Aaron Harwood, who worked in the New South Wales police force, would pop by every now and then and ask her to look after certain items, or sometimes large amounts of cash. This had proved to be quite a handy little arrangement as it always paid handsomely, money she used for trips abroad and the finer things in life. She preferred to keep this arrangement from Luke, after all what harm could it do? As far as he was concerned she earns good money as a part-time model and dancer. And that was just how she wanted to keep it. And then she began to think of Luke. Smiling as she lay back waiting for her man to come home, she placed her hands between her legs and began touching herself intimately, anticipating the moment when Luke arrived so they could make love until the morning.

Side by side, Luke and Monks casually walked to the exit of The Hero of Waterloo bar. Nobody dared try to stop them.

Monks snarled at anyone who so much as looked in their direction. He was buzzing, hoping somebody would be brave enough to try to stop them leaving because he was not yet satisfied – Monks wanted to damage somebody else. He was having fun. Once they got outside, a police car came screeching around the corner. Calm as you like, they both walked away, trying to look innocent as they headed for Bradfield Highway. Drawn by the sound of sirens wailing, a crowd of people came out of the hotel – another police vehicle plus a paramedic team were now on the scene.

Luke and Monks were almost around the corner, just seconds from being safely away when a young girl who had witnessed the whole incident came outside screaming to the two nearest police officers and pointing at Luke and Monks: 'They're over there, those two – do you see them?' 'You two stop right there!' the burly officer shouted out.

'Run!' Luke yelled, and they flew at speed around the corner, the burly officer and his colleague in hot pursuit. Instinctively they split up – at least then one of them could get away. Luke was quick on his feet, but only for short distances – he anticipated the moment when he knew he would tire. Monks, on the other hand, may not have been as fast, but he had exceptional stamina. He could run all day if need be; he used to love running the marathon at school. Having made it to Argyle Street, Monks turned into Watson Road and lost his pursuer as he jogged into Observatory Park. He slowed down and easily disappeared close to the Sydney Observatory, where he stopped to catch his breath. He thought it best to hide out there for twenty minutes, before making himself visible to the public again.

Luke had headed off to a flying start a long way in front of the police officers. His heart by this point was pumping at ten to the dozen. The burly officer was in pursuit, while his colleague was on his radio asking for support. Already Luke had almost crossed under Bradfield Highway, sprinting down

Argyle Street towards The Rocks. He stopped briefly to see how much ground he had on the burly police officer. Would he still be on his tail? Luke was relieved to see he was losing track a fair way back in the distance. When he was almost at the corner of George Street he assessed that he would soon be in a safe area. Luke stopped running and slowed down to a walk. Watching the approaching crowds he began to regulate his demeanour, trying to remain calm while preparing to slip in and mingle with the bustling Sydney crowd down at The Rocks. It would be so easy to lose himself in the night amongst the thronging crowds but he had to get there soon as his lungs were feeling as if they were about to burst. He stopped to take a breather, presuming that he had by now lost the cops. Luke glided into the first restaurant he saw, casually checking his expression in the mirror next to the entrance. Nodding to the maître d' in a confident 'How are you?' sort of way he pointed at the bar; the maître d' obviously presumed Luke was indicating that he was meeting a guest there. The trick to this was to act ultra confident, as if he had been delayed. Of course, all Luke wanted to do was get freshened up in their amenities, sneak a lively drink, hang around for a little, let the heat cool down and then be on his way. He ordered a small brandy, smiled at the bartender then slid off to the washroom to clean up.

He checked his mobile phone: no missed calls. Placing his phone next to the washbasin he ran the cold-water tap. As the water ran into the basin he began washing his hands, then splashed the soothing, invigorating liquid onto his head and face. Feeling fortunate to have got away from the police, Luke took deep breaths to regain his energy, the cool water sharpening up his senses as it ran down his neck. He wondered why he never broke a sweat. Even when he had been taking vigorous exercise, he never had an issue with body odour or sweating at all, strange as it seemed. This was a huge advantage in a situation like this, as to look at Luke now you would not think that he had been doing anything more than sitting in a bar reading a newspaper. He took a paper towel and wiped any remaining moisture off his face and neck. He adjusted his clothing, damped down his hair and took one last look in the mirror. Feeling that he looked respectable he picked up his mobile phone, placed it in his left-hand jeans pocket and left the washroom.

Gesturing to the maître d', Luke returned to his seat at the bar. He slugged back his brandy and ordered another one. The bartender duly obliged. He felt it was probably a good time to make a move, as he was sure that he had lost his tail. He swirled the brandy glass from side to side and then knocked back the fine cognac. It burned as it hit the back of his throat and a warm sensation tickled his chest. He stood up as the maître d' approached him. Politely he put up his hand before he had the opportunity to speak. The maître d' looked slightly confused as Luke passed him by, only pausing briefly to place a $20 bill into his hand. 'Thank you very much, sir,' the bemused maître d' said as he saw what Luke had put in his palm. 'Always a pleasure to see you my man,' said Luke. Then he winked at the bartender as he left.

He stepped out onto the pavement and then pushed up his collar. No more than a short distance now until I get to Circular Quay, Luke thought. He figured that Monks would probably aim to meet up with him down at the quay as soon as it seemed viable. Luke began walking at a brisk pace, alert to the fact that the Old Bill might be watching nearby. He made his way through George Street as discreetly as he could, staying aware of who was about and studying the reactions of all the people who passed him by to see if any of them found his appearance a little strange. Luke mingled in and out of the thronging crowds, desperately trying to avoid any eye contact and blend in. Hearing a police siren wailing in the distance, he stopped to look around. No, they were not searching for him he decided, as he watched the vehicle drive on by to a separate incident. He was not far now from the Museum of Contemporary Art and could see Circular Quay and the Cahil Expressway. A huge ship was docked next to Circular Quay, blocking the view of the Sydney Opera House, which would be looking magnificent at this time of night. As Luke approached the Circular Quay ferry terminal, he looked up in awe at the gigantic ship. Written on its side was '*Queen Mary 2*'. Must have a few spare pennies to sail on that big bastard, he thought as he passed on by.

Shannon jolted bolt upright, suddenly awake. She had dozed off for three hours or maybe more. It was dark now – the vibrant sound of people chattering and laughing below on the promenade must have startled her. She was feeling muzzy after waking and was in a half-asleep, half-awake state of mind. Shannon sat up on the chaise longue, wondering what the time could be and called out to see if her man was home. Silence reigned. She went inside the apartment to double check; it was now ten-thirty at night. No missed calls on her phone. Shannon did not want to bother Luke – let him have a night out, she thought, we always spend a lot of time together. It will do him good to cut loose with his old friend from England. Then she remembered with whom he had gone out on the town. There was definitely something wrong with Luke's old acquaintance – she did not like him. Maybe it was because he had tried it on with her more than once when she first met him in London. Even in the short time he had been in Australia, Monks had made Shannon feel uneasy, as if he was constantly leering at her. She certainly would not wish to spend too much time alone with him. She had yet to tell Luke any of this, as she knew the high regard in which Luke held his friend Monks. Shannon did not wish Luke to concern himself with these occurrences as she reckoned that if it came to anything she would be able to handle it without too much hassle. Although Shannon trusted Luke one hundred percent, she had noticed a slight change in Luke's behaviour every now and then when he was in Monks' company. The sooner Monks moved on the better, as far as Shannon was concerned.

She went to the kitchen, opened up the refrigerator and grabbed hold of a bottle of chilled Pinot Grigio. Collecting a large wine glass, she then picked up her packet of cigarettes and went back outside to listen to the sounds of Manly Beach. Now it was late at night, she was beginning to worry about Luke, but she tried to put her anxiety out of her mind. She was just hoping that Luke would be all right. Shannon proceeded to light another cigarette and walked to the edge of the balcony. She looked out over the promenade, and sat listening to waves breaking on the shore. She took a long, deep drag of her cigarette and tried to relax.

6

Modelling on Her Own

England

The day after their lads' night out, Luke was at work in the shop and feeling ropey. He glanced at the clock above the cigarettes: half past one. Only half an hour to wait until his Uncle Darren was due in to relieve him. He smiled as he remembered that he would be meeting up with Shannon later on. He'd had a cracking night out with the boys and got in around 2 a.m., meaning that he had got up to open the shop after a meagre three and a half hours sleep. Still, he would get four more hours when he finished up at work and then he should be as right as rain for his big date that evening.

Uncle Darren arrived just after two o' clock. 'Did you hear about the suspicious deaths last night, over at White City?' he asked Luke.

'Yes, a few customers have been talking about it in the shop today,' Luke responded.

'One of them was beaten to death in a flat and the other thrown out of a fourth-floor window,' Darren went on. 'What's it all coming to, Luke?'

'I really don't know, Uncle Darren.'

He sighed to Luke, and then walked out the back to make a cup of tea. After about five minutes Uncle Darren came into the front of the shop, took a swig of his tea, then said to Luke, 'Thanks for opening up earlier – you can shoot off now, and I'll see you Monday morning.'

'Cheers,' said Luke, grinning. 'Can I have my wages?'

'Of course, I've left your money out the back by the safe.'

'All right then, see you.' Luke went out the back, picked up his money and left to go home.

He decided to pop into the local for a swift half en route. As he pulled up outside, Monks was just leaving, chatting with a bloke Luke had never seen before. Luke parked up and strolled towards the public bar, passing Monks on the way in. 'All right, Monks – what time did you get in?'

'Too late – listen, I'll be in there in a minute, I'm just sorting out a bit of business.'

Luke still did not recognise the man he was talking to, and was a little unsure whether he wanted to either. 'Okay, I'll be having a game of pool and a bite to eat, see you in a bit.' Who the hell was Monks dealing with? Oh well, he thought, and carried on into his local.

Meanwhile, up near the West End, Shannon was getting ready for her interview. The man on the phone had told her to bring a change of clothes and a two-piece swimsuit for the shoot. She selected a classic black dress and a skimpy white bikini set; she had a terrific body, so she may as well show it off. After checking she had packed all the right gear, she took a shower before setting off to the address in Soho. She got on the Tube and made her way to a road just off Wardour Street. She found the dingy-looking basement not quite where she thought it would be – it did not have a good vibe about it, and it certainly was not glamorous. But she was here now, so she might as well give it a go. The door was already open so she pushed it a little further and was greeted by a short fat man. He introduced himself as Rory and explained that he was the director she had spoken to on the phone the previous day. He seemed friendly enough, she thought, although the venue selected for the shoot was slightly eerie, and it did not smell too fresh, either.

'Please, come through, come through,' he repeated. Shannon followed him into a large dimly lit room. Another man was standing in the corner of the room messing around with two separate cameras. He was mumbling away about something or other, she could not make out what he was saying; he had not even noticed that she had come into the room with Rory.

Shannon was then presented with a waiver form, and asked why she needed to sign it. 'Oh, nothing to worry about – just a couple of legal documents, it's not a big deal,' said Rory. Although this did not entirely convince her, Shannon decided to sign it anyway. He smiled as she signed, and then he asked her to change in the small room at the back of the building while they set up all the camera angles. As she changed into her little black dress with the skimpy white bikini underneath she saw her image in the mirror that sat in the corner. Pleased with what she could see, Shannon took a deep breath and left the tiny bathroom. When she came back out into the room, the two men were waiting, ready for action. The camera operator commented on her appearance. 'That all looks great, let's take some shots.' She felt reassured – they seemed professional, and she relaxed for the time being.

Shannon strolled under the spotlights and soon forgot about the grotty surroundings as they began taking a number of glamorous photographs. Both of them flattered Shannon repeatedly, telling her how professional and experienced she seemed, slowly drawing her in and making her feel first class. These two were good – they knew how to exploit the situation. After twenty minutes, they took a break.

'That will do for now,' said Rory. 'Let's take five and have a drink, then how about the swimwear session?'

'I'll take a drink then get changed,' agreed Shannon.

'Great, see you in a bit.'

Believing all was going well, Shannon walked back to the tiny bathroom to strip down. When she came out ten minutes later, the lights were much brighter than before, and she could just make out Rory, who by this time was controlling the camera. The other man, who hadn't told her his name, was out of sight.

'Just keep on walking towards the lights, honey,' said Rory.

Shannon now felt foolish in her white two-piece bikini set and high-heeled shoes. Then, out from the side came the other man. It sank in immediately when she saw him, tall and powerfully built, in just a pair of tight black boxer shorts that were far too small for him. He pushed her over to a large black office style table with four different mirrors positioned for altered angles of what they intended to film that evening. So stupid, she thought – she had told no one where she was and had left herself completely vulnerable to the situation. 'Now then, let's shoot some proper action,' said Muscles, grabbing hold of her and bending her over the desk. Rory moved across to them both with the camera, filming it all. 'You have got a career in this type of work, if you want it,' he said, mocking her.

The room was locked and it would be pointless to scream for help, even though she was in the heart of Soho – on entering the building she did not recall seeing anyone else around. Shannon, by now panicking, knew she was in a lot of difficulty. 'There's a good girl, just act as if you are enjoying yourself,' continued Rory. As Muscles held her arms behind her back with one hand, he pulled down his boxer shorts with the other. She could feel his growing erection pushing into the small of her back. Rory had manoeuvred himself in front of her, still filming everything. He had two cameras working on tripods. It was set up perfectly – Shannon had been well and truly duped. They had cajoled her into wearing a skimpy bikini, completely taken her in with a few compliments here and there, and the worse thing of all was she had signed a consent form earlier. How dumb could she be? It was a complete fraud from the beginning; get a silly girl to try for a modelling interview in her underwear, in a near-deserted building. Get her to smile and look like she is having fun, then both of the scammers take it in turns to rape and abuse her. After all, she had given her signature on a contract to say that she was a willing participant in a gang rape porno movie, so who was going to believe her if she said otherwise? The chances are the poor girl would never tell anyone of her nightmare. They had it watertight – how many times had they done this type of thing before? The bastards – this fraud seemed foolproof. 'Come on, sweetheart – you may as well enjoy it, because you are not going anywhere until we are done,' Rory said, laughing as he stripped off his jeans and briefs. His fat belly hung in front of her face and he held his flaccid penis in his hand as he whispered, 'Open your mouth and work the shaft of my cock – make sure you swallow the contents.'

All of a sudden, her survival instincts began to kick in. All the experience of her miserable childhood had come in to play. She was brought up in a children's home back in Sydney, where perverted carers abused a select few. 'The special ones', they used to call them. She learnt a thing or two in there, and trying to avoid regular sexual abuse was one of them. It taught her some valuable lessons in life. Her best friend who she grew up with in there suddenly came into her mind – she remembered how they protected each other in those horrific days and nights of physical and mental abuse. Somehow, they got through it together. She was certainly not going to let anyone else violate her again, not these two pricks – no way.

She knew she had to look as if she was compliant to their demands. Just bide your time, she told herself. She felt

Muscles' huge erection in-between her thighs as he eagerly massaged her out-of-this-world backside. She could feel him slowly start to peel off her bikini bottoms. Shannon felt surprisingly calm as she waited for the right moment. 'That's right, darling, just relax – we are going to have some fun tonight.' Determined not to let them think that she was going to struggle she fluttered her eyes at Rory. He grinned, and then spoke to his fellow would-be rapist, 'We're ready for action.' Muscles released his tight grip on Shannon's arm, giving her vital seconds to react. Shannon's head started spinning, her arm feeling numb from where he had pinned it to her back. No time to worry about that now – this could be her only chance.

Muscles was still fondling her buttocks – he had not yet pulled her bottoms completely down. Rory held open her mouth, with his half-erect penis in his hand. He moved his penis close to her mouth, as the muscular man released her from her bikini bottoms. It's time to make them pay, thought Shannon, and in that split second she bit down as hard as she could on the tip of Rory's penis and in one swift movement she threw her head back as powerfully as possible. The back of her head smashed straight into Muscles' nose, breaking it instantly. He stumbled back, putting his hands to his face, blood seeping through them. She had caught him perfectly, giving her more valuable seconds for her escape. She spat a mouthful of warm blood and gristle out. Rory was on his knees in agony. Stepping to one side she was feeling amazingly calm. In fact, she was buzzing – she was in complete control.

Muscles was angry. Shaking his head and clenching his fists he strode towards her. He knew he was physically stronger than she was and he was planning to hurt her real bad. 'I'm going to kick the shit out of you, and rape the fuck out of you over and over,' he threatened. Shannon kicked off her high-heeled shoes, pushed the large digital camera off its tripod, and with all her strength swung the tripod at his nose. It connected sweetly, knocking the man clean off his feet. As the adrenaline kicked in, she cracked the tripod down onto his head twice more; hearing it smash into his skull was satisfying.

Turning to look at Rory, who was on his knees holding his testicles and whimpering like a beaten puppy, she realised that what she had spat out of her mouth was the tip of Rory's cock. She took a couple of deep breaths, and then decided that she was not yet finished with these two filthy rapists. She laughed as she observed Rory's plight. He was moaning in agony in a pathetic display of mourning for his now even smaller cock. 'Not having as much fun as you thought you might be?' she taunted.

She went back over to where Muscles lay to pick up the now bent tripod. It felt a lot heavier now she had calmed down. She looked at Muscles; he lay entirely still. Had she killed him? She was not sure, and if she had, she could not care less. With the tripod in her arms, Shannon walked across to Rory, who was still on his knees. His face was almost devoid of any colour at all; he looked drained and extremely weak as he had lost so much blood from what was left of his penis. He was cupping his genitals with both hands, as if frightened to look at the damage which she had done. She picked up her torn swimwear. Shannon was almost entirely naked but for her bikini top.

'Please help me – get me to hospital,' Rory whimpered.

Unbelievable, she thought. 'You and your friend were going to fuck me against my will, now you want me to help you.'

'Please, I'll do anything – money, whatever you want. Please, I'm begging you.'

Shannon stood there for moments listening to him plead for help. Suddenly she felt cold. 'I want you to bleed to death, you dirty fucking bastard.'

Shannon turned with the tripod and her tattered swimwear in her hand and walked to the tiny bathroom to put on her clothes. As she walked away, she wiggled her fabulous buttocks so that Rory, with half a penis and in unbearable agony, could see what he did not manage to enjoy, and probably never would ever again.

She dressed as quickly as possible, keeping the door ajar so she could monitor the two scumbags in the main room. When she returned, Rory had managed to crawl to where he thought the tip of his cock would be, but the amount of blood he'd lost had left him exhausted. Muscles began to groan. Shannon moved quickly to him and hit him with the tripod to keep him quiet. She then went across the room and smashed up all the cameras and equipment, removed all the memory sticks and put them in her pockets. She spoke to the half-conscious Rory: 'I enjoyed that – we must do it again some time.' With that, she hit him in the testicles with the broken tripod. He yelped out in pain. She left the building and walked back to Soho, throwing the memory sticks down a fast-running drain nearby.

Shannon entered a pub not far from where she was due to meet Luke later on that night. She smiled at the barman and went straight into the toilets. As soon as she'd locked the cubicle door she sat down on the seat and began to weep, all the pain and anguish pouring out of her. She could not stop her tears.

7

Circular Quay to Manly

Sydney

Luke had been ultra cautious before arriving at the Circular Quay ferry terminal, but he was now beginning to feel relieved as he went across to the departures board to check how long he would have to wait until the next ferry to Manly Beach. He would only have to hang around for ten minutes as it turned out, as the ferry was already loading with passengers. Still no sign of Monks. He looked at the timetable once more, then he walked across to the sales booth to hand over the fee to the miserable old man sitting behind the ticket window. Checking his mobile phone again, Luke decided to board the ferry; Monks would just have to catch him up at a later point. Luke stepped onto the gangplank behind a sweet elderly couple. He helped the gent lift his wife on board, as she looked quite frail and not too stable on her feet. 'Thank you, young man,' she said, and the old gent smiled at Luke. 'No problem at all,' Luke replied. Walking to the top of the gangplank, he took one last look back down at the ferry terminal; nobody was getting on after him. The stewards signalled to each other then began closing the safety barriers. The captain of the ferry came over the PA system to announce information on the short crossing across the harbour, to which Luke did not pay any attention. Making his way to the top deck of the vessel he passed the elderly couple again, and nodded and smiled at the sweet old pair.

The journey from Circular Quay to Manly Cove is only a 7-mile trip. Luke was starting to relax now, knowing he was close to relative safety, away from the evening's earlier mayhem that had been created by Monks in The Hero of Waterloo. I won't be welcome back there any time soon, he thought. He sat down near the front of the ferry so he could watch the water below while listening to the commentary that ran throughout the crossing. He always enjoyed taking in the view of Sydney Harbour, especially the Sydney Opera House, which was beautifully lit up in the dark. Luke stood up and moved to the back of the deck so he could watch the opera house slowly disappear behind him. The ferry was not even a third full. Luke went to buy a soft drink, but the confectionery stall was not open, presumably because there were so few passengers travelling on the later transportation. Luke's mobile phone was starting to vibrate in his jeans pocket. He pulled it out to see that it was a text message. It will probably be Monks, he thought, letting me know that he is in a police cell or on his way back home. To Luke's surprise, the text came from Shannon. 'Thinking about you hon, hope you're having fun. LOVE YOU.' Strange, thought Luke, as they rarely sent each other soppy text messages. Still, Luke replied to her: 'On the way home, catch you soon.'

An announcement came over on the PA system: 'We will shortly be arriving at Manly Wharf. Would you please make sure that you take all your belongings with you.' Luke went down the stairs to the lower deck. He walked up to the sweet elderly couple and asked if the woman would be requiring a hand as they departed the vessel. She politely declined, explaining, 'I'm all right going down the steps, darling, it's going up them that I struggle. Thank you for your concern.' Luke smiled at the sweet old woman, waved, then passed them by. He was pleased to have offered to help them – his family would be proud of how Luke had never forgotten that you should always respect your elders and lend a helping hand wherever you can. After all, it costs nothing to show civility and to have good manners. Whatever else happened in life, Luke took a lot of pride believing that he had been brought up correctly and that he behaved with a great deal of class. He stumbled forwards as the ferry docked with a shudder at the smart, rejuvenated Manly Wharf. Luke held onto the railings to maintain his balance. That must have been the bumpiest docking he had ever experienced – was the captain drunk? He turned round to make sure his elderly friends were okay. They waved at Luke to assure him that they were fine. He put up his hand as a gesture of farewell then stepped off the ferry onto terra firma, glanced to the right and smiled into the glare of the lights that were constantly flashing at the Manly Wharf amusement park.

Meanwhile, the burly uniformed officer, whose name was Harwood, had returned to The Hero of Waterloo with his partner Mills, or 'Milo', as everybody called him. He was bent over double, recovering from giving chase to the two suspects. Breathing in and out, Harwood took off his cap, wiped his brow and regained his composure. 'Okay, Milo, what do we know?'

'The victim is not feeling too clever, mate, there's a lot of blood, and the paramedics are trying to clean him up a bit.'

'Any witnesses?' Harwood asked.

Milo looked quizzically at Harwood. 'A whole bloody pub, mate.'

Two other inexperienced police officers were now taking statements from punters who were standing outside. Harwood wanted to deal with it himself, so he went across to relieve his colleagues of their duties. 'It's okay, boys – I'm on this one.' The two officers nodded and left Harwood to it.

Inside the pub the heavily built man was still bleeding profusely. A young paramedic and her expert team were aiding him. His lean wiry pal, who had given his name to the police officers as 'Dave', was walking with a limp as his bollocks were still aching. He stood nearby waiting for some attention, sure that he had a couple of broken ribs.

'Is Paul going to be okay?' asked Dave in a high-pitched tone, indicating his injured friend.

'Just give us some room to do our job,' the young paramedic replied. The team placed Paul's badly swollen head gently into a brace and strapped it in place to keep it from moving. They were trying to stem the flow of blood that was still pouring from his head.

'I've been injured too, you know, is anyone going to help me out?' said Dave, feeling sorry for his friend but also looking for a little sympathy for his aching ribs and balls. But the paramedics were far too concerned for the man on the floor, as his condition was worsening rapidly, whereas Dave's injuries were only superficial.

'Who here can tell me what happened in here tonight? Because no one is going home until I find out,' Harwood said as he entered The Hero of Waterloo, surveying the crime scene inside.

Dave piped up straight away, 'Yeah mate, the bastards attacked me too.'

Harwood beckoned him over. As Dave spoke to Harwood he watched as four paramedics struggled to lift and carry the huge weight of his friend out to the waiting ambulance on a stretcher. He explained to Harwood that the man on the stretcher was his friend. His ribs and testicles seemed to be throbbing in harmony. 'I need some help, I'm in a fair bit of pain, mate,' he said, still waiting for a little attention, but none was forthcoming. It seems that nobody is the slightest bit interested in making sure my nuts have not been rearranged to sit up in my windpipe, he thought.

'No worries, just give me a statement, and we'll get you sorted, mate,' said Harwood, who did not really give a shit. The stupid fucker can wait a while, he thought, even though the chap was quite clearly in a great deal of pain and duly concerned that his mate was in a serious condition. He was a mean, vicious copper, who had no time for anybody stupid enough to get him or herself hurt in a pointless brawl. The only reason he was even the slightest bit interested in this incident was because the two suspects had given him the slip. That fact alone had Harwood's blood boiling; there was nothing that he and his partner Milo enjoyed more than tracking down any cheeky bastard who thought they could pull one over on them.

'So, in your own time, describe to me what happened,' he said. Dave shakily explained the events of the evening to Harwood, who in turn worked out immediately that this lean wiry fool was certainly not as innocent as he would like to portray.

Milo stepped inside to speak to Harwood. 'The fat bastard is in a bad way,' Milo quipped – not a very tactful comment to make right in front of the man's pal. Neither of them were the most sensitive of souls – perhaps that was why they made such a good team. They couldn't care less about the stupid victims, as they saw it. However, they did like to hand out their own special form of criminal justice when pursuing so-called villains. And Harwood really fancied solving this one. 'That's my mate out there,' Dave said. 'Is he going to be all right?'

Milo, slightly embarrassed, looked at Harwood, who answered for him. 'He'll be all right mate; they'll take good care of him at the hospital.'

Harwood placed his arm on Dave's shoulder, and then said, 'Listen, you're obviously worried about your mate – go on, get in the ambulance and we'll follow you to the hospital in a minute.'

'Good on you, mate,' said Dave, and then limped out of the pub. One of the barmaids enquired if they could mop up all the blood, which covered a large area by now. Harwood told them that they could shut down the bar for the night as the forensic team were on their way and would need to section off the whole pub to maintain any evidence.

The paramedics were doing all they could to try to keep Paul breathing normally; they had to get him to hospital as quickly as possible. His pal climbed into the vehicle to sit next to him. They slammed the doors shut behind him and the ambulance raced away, sirens on and at full speed.

Monks had left the sanctuary of Observatory Park a good while earlier and walking along at a quick pace was almost in the city. As he turned the corner into George Street, an ambulance sped past; he panicked, realising the Old Bill would be near. He had to be discreet. He swerved into a couple of young girls, asking them the time, making it look to the police car almost directly behind the ambulance that he was in a group on a night out. Harwood was in the passenger seat on his radio. He glanced out of the window and looked straight at Monks as they whizzed past. Monks had placed his head at an angle on one of the girl's shoulders and was cracking one of his corny jokes. He could feel Harwood staring at him; it all happened in a flash. Harwood had a strange feeling that he had just missed something. Monks felt exactly the same.

Sitting next to his mate on the way to the hospital, Dave had become quite concerned as it began to dawn on him that his own ailments were irrelevant by comparison. The paramedics were constantly swabbing his friend's head. He had not been able to move for a while, and it seemed perfectly clear that Paul would be fortunate to pull through this incident unscathed. Moving a heavily built man with severe head injuries who is still motionless is not an easy task, and the paramedics operated with the utmost care and attention to move him out of the ambulance once they arrived at the hospital, before rushing him through to A&E.

The police arrived seconds behind the ambulance. With Milo following him, Harwood caught up with Dave. 'Hey, we need to speak with you further'.

'Sure, anything you say,' said Dave. The man had tears welling up in his eyes.

Milo said, 'Let's speak to the paramedics, to get an update on this bloke's condition first.'

'Okay, you go in; I'll stay here with this chap and have a little chat,' replied Harwood.

With his vast expertise in these situations, Harwood managed to relax Dave. He escorted him to a quiet room inside the hospital to finish taking down his statement.

Inside, the nurses had wired Paul up to all sorts of monitors and tubes and transferred him straight to the operating theatre, where the surgeon was desperately trying to stop the blood clotting on the brain.

Milo waited outside the operating theatre, chatting up one of the nurses who was taking a break.

'What time do you knock off, darling?'

'I'm pulling an all-nighter; I won't be finished until six.'

'How about if I pick you up and take you for a coffee after you're done here, what do you say?'

'You're a fast mover,' she said, then smiled at him. 'I tell you what; let me give you my mobile number and you can give me a call tomorrow while I think about it.'

Milo smiled back at her. He took the paper she had written down her number on and put it in his pocket. The nurse's pager beeped then and she walked away, turning to give Milo a cute wave as she disappeared around the corner. Another notch on the bedpost with a bit of luck, he thought.

Two hours later, the surgeons were still operating on Paul, doing the best they could to save him from living the rest of his life in a vegetative state. Dr Robb was a brilliant surgeon, though even he would have to admit that the signs for this patient did not look great.

While surgery continued, the nurse Milo had been trying to arrange a date with had been instructed to contact Paul's next of kin. She went to the quiet room to ask Harwood for any information that he might have, and Dave was able to divulge all the necessary details.

'His sister's name is Kerry Symonds – I will call her for you,' said Dave.

'Thank you,' said the nurse, turning to leave.

A phone call and an hour later, Kerry arrived at the hospital.

8

Meeting Danny Chilton

England

Luke was at home preparing for his date with Shannon. After getting dressed and sharing a cup of tea with his mum and brother, he left the house. As he sauntered through the streets of Shepherd's Bush to make his way to the Tube he noticed that a baby-blue Bentley had started following him as soon as he turned the corner from his house. He half recognised the vehicle from earlier in the day when he had popped in the pub after work. It was most definitely keeping close to him as he got nearer to the Underground station. Luke tried to walk a touch quicker to see if he was not just being paranoid about it. While Luke kept on glancing round to see if they were still in pursuit, he bumped into a young teenage couple who responded with a bad attitude. 'Watch where you're going, you dick,' the aggressive and clearly perturbed young male of the two said, at which Luke laughed and told the wannabe bad man clearly, 'Fuck off, before I give you a slap.' The aggressive teenager looked Luke up and down.

At that precise moment the Bentley pulled up right next to them. Pug the co-driver swung open the door and stood in front of the teenagers. 'Move on, before you get hurt,' he barked. The teenagers were stunned to see this big man jump out of nowhere and they scuttled off without saying another word. Luke was just as confused as they must have been.

'Who the fuck are you then – some sort of superhero?' he said.

'Don't try to be clever, Luke. Get in the car, son. Danny would like a chat.'

'Danny? I don't know a Danny,' Luke objected. 'Who –'

'Just get in the car, I won't ask you again,' said the man abruptly.

Luke looked in the back seat of the Bentley and recognised the man he'd seen talking to his Uncle Darren the previous week. Considering this, Luke thought it might be wise to have that chat with him.

Danny Chilton, sitting comfortably in the back seat, offered Luke his hand in friendship. Being well brought up Luke duly obliged, but he knew sitting in the back of a car owned by Danny Chilton for a chat in West London on a Saturday night could not be good news, surely.

'I won't keep you long, Luke. I just want to ask one or two questions,' Danny explained.

Looking at the front seat, Luke noticed that Danny's brother Jack was not with him, which was unusual as the two of them were always together on a Saturday.

'Sure, Danny, what's up?'

'An acquaintance of mine who knows your family very well was telling me that you and your pal are doing all right in the mobile phone game.'

Luke was not sure how to answer this enquiry. Did he deny all knowledge, or just butter Danny up a bit and hope that he would soon lose interest?

'Yeah, we make a quid or two now and then,' Luke admitted.

'I hear it's more than a couple of quid, Luke.'

'Well, you know …'

Why was a major player like Danny Chilton so interested? He had a finger in every swindle in West London. That is why, Luke thought – he wanted to be involved. Or, knowing this man's reputation, he wanted to take over their profitable sideline. Luke continued to play dumb.

'Okay, we can make two hundred a go sometimes.'

'Don't try to fob me off with that shit, son,' said Danny tersely.

'No, honest – it's not that great.'

Danny looked pissed off. 'Right, you little prick, I'm coming into your uncle's shop next Friday.'

Luke started to feel slightly nauseous. He knew exactly what this horrible bastard wanted.

'When I come in to visit, I want a thousand pounds.'

Luke swallowed hard. Danny and his mob were going to take all their profits and there was nothing he and Monks could do about it.

'Now get out of my fucking motor, I'll see you on Friday.'

The car stopped almost a mile from the Tube station Luke needed. Luke opened the door and got out, then watched the Bentley speed off. Once the motor was out of sight, he took out his mobile phone and gave Monks a call.

'Hello mate, we've got a big problem.'

An hour later, Luke was standing outside a pub in the West End to meet his date. He was not a regular smoker, but as he was feeling nervous he lit a cigarette. He only took a couple of drags and put it out before popping a mint into his mouth. He looked at his watch to check that he was not too early: he was bang on time.

Shannon had been back to her small flat and changed for the evening. She was looking forward to meeting Luke and had calmed down from the day's tumultuous events. She had arrived early at the bar as she needed a stiff drink to try to block out the memory of the Rory and Muscles show. She'd found a nice cosy seat in the snug and had been sipping her vodka and coke and trying to unwind for a while until Luke was due to arrive. Now, on her way back from the ladies', she spotted him straight away as he entered the pub. Luke turned after feeling a tap on the shoulder. Shannon, relieved to see a friendly face after her nightmare that day, smiled, grabbed hold of him and kissed him. Luke grinned like a Cheshire cat at her passionate embrace, thinking to himself that maybe this wasn't such a bad day after all.

Shannon seemed to respond to Luke's good sense of humour – he made her laugh. They stayed up west for the most part of the evening and then ended up back at her tiny bedsit south of the river in Bermondsey. It worked out that they had so much in common. Her quick wit and sense of fun seemed to instantly appeal to Luke's similar likes and dislikes. Though still feeling numb from her dangerous and disastrous modelling tryout, Shannon blocked it all out for now so she could enjoy Luke's company. Funnily enough, Luke was also reeling from his conversation with Danny Chilton, but as they were both falling for each other's charms none of the shit they were going through seemed to matter. Following what had happened in Soho, Shannon was feeling vulnerable and, for the first time in months, so alone. She knew as soon as she set eyes upon Luke that he was a good man. It was as if they had known each other forever, the bond seemed instant. Hence, early on in the evening Shannon was certain that she would be sleeping with him that night. The passionate kiss they shared as they met had set a spark in the pair of them.

'You would love Sydney, Luke.'

A strange thing to say, thought Luke, that came from nowhere.

'I've never really thought about going there,' he replied.

Shannon had made up her mind that she was going home as soon as possible. She had managed to hold onto a large amount of cash, from her friend back in Australia, and put away a fair bit of money while she had been staying in London. The fact that she may have killed two potential rapists that day made her think it might be wise to disappear in the near future. Tonight, though, she knew she needed to be with a good man.

'Perhaps you can show me Sydney one day,' said Luke, continuing what to him seemed a random line of conversation. Shannon smiled; she felt safe.

'I'll be back in a minute,' she said.

Luke smiled back then took a sip of his lager. Shannon went out of the room for a short while. Luke looked around the small living room, which was tastefully decorated. He thought it strange that he could not see any pictures of her family anywhere. You could not walk two centimetres in his house without seeing a picture of him, his brother, or all three of them together at home. Maybe my mother is the only one who likes to go overboard and fill every space with family photos, he thought, chuckling to himself. Luke sat back down on the sofa, waiting for Shannon to come back.

When Shannon returned to the living room, she was wearing a silk robe and very little underneath. Luke's eyes nearly popped out of his head. They were getting on famously well, but he didn't think it would move onto the next level so fast. He could feel a stirring in his loins as he could make out her silhouette under the blue robe that barely covered her ample bosom. Her curves were incredible – she has a stunning body, he thought. Moving towards Luke, she seductively sat in front of him. She wanted him so badly. To forget the misery of the modelling tryout she needed to feel loved, not abused.

Luke shifted nervously; she had caught him unawares. As he went to speak she put her finger to his mouth as if to silence him. Shannon rose up, gently held his hands, moved forwards and kissed him frivolously on the mouth. Luke responded to her kiss as they both stood up. His hands roamed around her shoulders, lifting her robe off. It dropped to the floor. Shannon was completely naked, except for the high-heeled shoes that she had worn earlier to the ill-fated tryout. Luke admired her magnificent figure as her hands moved over his fine physique. He took off his shirt to reveal his well-toned torso and chest, then undid his belt and pulled down his jeans. Luke's manhood was fully erect as her hands brushed past. He kissed her fervently as she slowly began to massage his excited manhood. 'Take me, Luke, I need you right now,' she said breathlessly.

Luke was a more than willing participant. He held her in his arms and lifted her perfectly firm buttocks in his hands. They lost themselves in the throes of passion as he entered her in one swift movement. Pushing her up against the wall he began thrusting with wild fervour. They moaned in sync as if they were one. It was so intense as he pumped harder and faster, kissing her neck as he tried to contain his pleasure. It felt like forever in the moment. Luke could feel the excitement rapidly building as they were nearing orgasm. Shannon groaned as Luke exploded inside her; they came together. The intensity released, they fell onto the sofa, puffing and panting and out of breath. Shannon held Luke tighter than she had ever held anyone before. In only one night, Shannon had fallen head over heels in love. As Luke admired her superb figure, he too had become completely besotted.

Meanwhile, Monks was in conversation with the chap he had been talking to earlier, when Luke passed him in the afternoon. For a while now he had been trying to become involved with a small outfit with connections in the world of dealing pills and cocaine. The trouble with this plan was that the people he was knocking about with were also quite friendly with the Chilton mob, and they regularly had to report all sorts of information back to the main man. Little did Monks know that he was about to have a polite conversation with Danny Chilton himself.

'Hello Monks, how are you?' said Danny as he walked into Monks' local with a couple of heavy minders.

'Not too bad, Danny, thanks. You?'

Monks had already been warned by Luke that Danny was taking an interest in them.

'Take a walk with me, son,' Danny said.

The pub was only half full – unusual for a Saturday night – but most of the regular drinkers were looking into their glasses, trying not to make any eye contact with Danny or his minders. Monks realised that he had no choice but to go with him.

'I suppose your accomplice has already spoken to you.'

Monks feigned slight surprise, and raised his eyebrows. 'No, what do you mean?'

Danny shook his head and laughed. 'Listen, and listen well: be at your boy's shop on Friday.'

Monks knew that there was not a lot more he could say. He nodded and then said to Danny, 'Sorry, Luke did ring me, but to be honest –'

'I said just be there on Friday with the money,' Danny interrupted.

Monks decided not to say anything for now, even though he had to bite his tongue. He was in no way scared of Danny Chilton; the truth was he hated him. However, Monks knew that he just had to bide his time, and he intended to play it cool just for a week or so. Monks pretended that he was in awe of him. I will sort you out, you bastard, he thought to himself. Just you fucking wait – this is not over, by a long way. Danny looked pleased, as he had not yet worked Monks out. Of course, he presumed that he would soon have these two mugs in his pocket.

'Yeah, sorry Danny, I will be there, I wasn't trying to be rude.'

Monks despised this moment, but he had to act as if he were afraid. Danny, satisfied that he was in complete control, tapped Monks on the left cheek, trying to gauge his reaction, 'You know it's the right thing to do.'

Rixon, the driver, smirked at Monks as they turned to leave. When they had left, Monks walked back to the bar and looked around. Nobody had yet even glanced over in his direction. A good job, too, as Monks was furious and ready to kick the shit out of the first person who happened to catch his eye. He ordered a pint of lager. As the barmaid poured his drink she asked, 'Are you okay, love? You look a little upset.' Monks stared at her. His eyes pierced right through her. 'Just pour me the fucking drink,' he spat. The pub remained silent.

9

Safe and Sound

Sydney

Luke called Shannon on his mobile phone as he strolled down Manly Wharf promenade.

'Hey sweetheart, I've just got off the ferry. I should be home in five minutes.'

'Okay, Luke. I'll pour you a nice cool drink, honey, see you soon.'

He ended the call and went to put the phone back in his pocket, but it started ringing again. He answered thinking it was Shannon.

'Where did you go mate?' said Monks' gruff voice down the line.

'I'm in Manly. Did you give the Old Bill the slip?' Luke asked.

'Of course,' Monks snapped. 'I wouldn't be talking to you if I hadn't.'

'All right, mate – where are you staying tonight?'

'No problems there, mate – a little hostel in King's Cross.'

'Good. Keep your head down.'

'Listen, I'll give you a bell in the morning.'

'Cool, see you then.'

'Yeah, see you later,' said Monks.

Luke knew that Monks would be fine. He turned the

corner onto the beachfront where their handsome apartment was located. Luke would often entertain himself by people watching; he could sit down in a restaurant or a bar, find a comfortable spot inside or out, and spend hours on end observing the features and mannerisms of all the different types of characters as they passed on by going about their daily routines. It never failed to amuse him, trying to imagine why they were all rushing around and what they were thinking. He liked to think that he could tell what type of people they were by the way they were walking or how they were dressed. Human nature truly fascinated him. Only a short distance from the apartment building it seemed he may have to put his observational skills to the test, as four very drunk or drugged up teenagers were about to cross his path. As he got closer Luke could clearly see that these lads would be no bother. They were all just in very high spirits, thankfully; the last thing Luke needed now would be any more grief tonight. One of the lads stumbled into Luke's path.

'Sorry, mate,' one of his friends said to Luke. 'He's had too much.'

Luke smiled at the lads, held up his hand and said, 'I just hope you get him home in one piece.'

'Yeah, mate, so do we.'

Another of the lads wished Luke a nice evening. Luke returned the gesture then watched them continue down the street on their way to another bar. He figured that they were a decent group of lads. They struggled to keep their friend from falling head over heels again and he laughed at the sight as he took out his key and walked up the steps to his apartment building. On entering the building, Luke stopped to exchange small talk with the night attendant. He could never remember his name, probably because the only time he ever bumped into him was when he was returning from a night out on the lash on the weekend and asked him his name on the way in, only to forget it by the morning when the hangover kicked in. Anyway, he seemed like a nice chap, Luke thought as he wished him goodnight and got into the elevator.

Luke pushed the button for the penthouse, leaning back onto the wall as the lift raced up to the top floor in no time at all. He thought it best not to mention to Shannon what had happened earlier that evening in The Hero of Waterloo. Shannon meant the world to him and he did not see the point in worrying her unduly. He hoped the victim from the pub would be okay after the vicious beating he had received, because he definitely did not look at all well when they left him lying motionless in his own blood on the bar room floor. Luke opened the front door of the apartment and pushed the memory of the heavily bleeding man to the back of his mind.

The lights were dim as he entered the hallway and walked through into the spacious lounge of the apartment. The French doors were open so he walked out onto the balcony. He felt the cool northerly breeze gently blowing onto his face. 'Shannon, I'm home.' There was no reply. A large cool drink was set up on the table next to a couple of flickering candles that were struggling to stay alight. He sat down in a chaise longue and took a long sip from the cocktail that Shannon had prepared for him. As he lay back onto the comfortable lounger and closed his eyes Shannon appeared on the balcony. 'Hey, baby,' she said. Luke opened his eyes, greeted by the sight of her standing in front of him in a short silk Versace robe that scarcely covered her waist and hugged her more than ample breasts tightly.

'Hi, honey, did you have a good time?' Not as good as I am about to, Luke thought as he stared at her voluptuous body. She seemed to shimmer with the moonlight as it helped to show off her incredible outline. 'You look beautiful, Shannon.' She smiled at him and then knelt down in front of him. Luke sat up as she slowly moved her hands along his inner thighs. Luke felt an erection form instantly as her hands neared the crotch of his jeans. Caressing his now fully erect penis through his jeans, she slowly teased him until Luke's fervour was raging for release. Shannon rose to her feet and delicately opened her robe, then let it drop little by little to the floor. She turned around so that Luke could see the full outlook of her stunning body, and then stepped just inside their apartment. In the twilight, Luke had an amazing view of Shannon's succulent ass. Glancing seductively over her shoulder she asked, 'Are you coming to bed?' Luke could barely contain his enthusiasm. She teasingly began walking through the lounge, clicking her high-heeled stilettos, with every step wiggling her gorgeous ass provocatively, knowing Luke would be watching her every move. As Luke got up to follow her upstairs into the bedroom, his erection was trying to burst out of his denims. As he got to the stairs, Shannon was already halfway up. All Luke could think of as he looked up was how much he wanted to get hold of her terrific body and fuck her until the sun came up.

Luke was now at the top of the stairs moving across to the bedroom. He just managed to get through the door when Shannon leapt at him and kissed him passionately. Responding to her Luke began kissing her neck, as he knew she adored it when he did this. Her hands ripped at his shirt, tearing off the buttons to reveal his muscular chest and torso. Her hands moved down to his waist, then she undid his belt and pulled down his jeans, pushing him onto the bed. Her naked body lay on top of him, and she moved down and slowly pulled off his boxer shorts. His penis was finally released, hard and ready, and she teased him a little more. Luke moaned as she took his erection into her mouth and slowly worked up and down the shaft, pleasuring Luke as he cried out even louder; he was not sure how long he would be able to contain his excitement as Shannon sucked on his hard aching cock.

*   *   *

Monks was nearing King's Cross in a taxi he had hailed from The Rocks after speaking to Luke, watching every move the cabbie was making closely. He did not trust taxi drivers; he always thought they were out to con him. The taxi driver did not seem too sure about Monks either, as he was babbling away in a foreign tongue. Monks had now become distracted by the ladies of the night who were showing their goods to all and sundry. Some of them were hardly covering anything up at all. Up by King's Cross he checked the fare and decided that he would take in the view. Then, asking the taxi driver to pull over by the working girls, he thought he would wind the man up. It was clear that he did not approve of the activities that Monks had on his mind. From the insignia that hung from the rear-view mirror of the taxi Monks knew the odds were that he was a man of faith. Monks hated all religion, due to a strict religious upbringing. As a young child he rebelled as soon as he was able. It didn't matter to him what faith people believed in; he despised them all. Seeing how uncomfortable this clearly moral family man felt, being requested to stop by the streetwalkers, he thought he would wind the cabbie up for a bit of sport.

'What's up, buddy? Don't you like to look at the pretty girls up here? Or maybe you are a faggot,' he said mockingly as the cabbie pulled over and tried not to look at the girls, who were now curious about a possible punter.

'Just pay the fare and leave my car please,' he said. A middle-aged and rather well-used-looking prostitute was approaching the vehicle. Monks, sensing the cabbie's discomfort, decided to taunt the man a tad more. He laughed as he said, 'Come on, my old mate, how about you and me spit roast this one? I'll pay and we can call it quits on the cab fare, what do you reckon?'

'I will not ask you again. Please leave the vehicle, or I will call the police.'

As Monks leant forward, taking out ten dollars, his frame of mind changed quite swiftly. His tone now became threatening; he wanted to frighten the completely innocent cabbie because he knew he could.

'Listen, I do not like being told what to do, especially by some fucking immigrant taxi driver, now here is ten bucks. That is all I am paying you, all right with that, son?'

The scared and very hesitant cabbie nodded, and then released the cab door. 'Good boy,' said Monks as he stepped out of the cab.

'Last chance, pal, I'll set it up for us, she's coming over,' he called out, amusing himself even more. The cabbie chose to ignore Monks' crude offer. Monks then slammed the cab door shut and the cabbie sped off, giving Monks the middle finger as he went. Well, that is not exactly peace to all men, is it? Monks thought as he waved sarcastically in the taxi's direction. The middle-aged prostitute approached him. 'Fuck off, you diseased old whore,' he screamed in the poor woman's face. Then he walked off laughing. Oh, how Monks was enjoying himself. He decided that he did fancy a little action before he went up to the youth hostel, which was just in the region of the inner-city suburb of Darlinghurst. Eyeing up a much younger, less used working girl he beckoned her over in to his path. In high heels that she struggled to walk in, the girl stumbled across to him, with a forced smile on her face. Monks gave her the once over as she got nearer. He'd had an eventful evening, so he was knackered, but he really fancied a blow job before he called it a night.

'You want some business, mister?' the young – in fact, maybe a little too young – girl asked him. Monks was aghast. He lightly put his arm around her shoulder, his appetite for receiving any sort of sexual favour quashed. It was obvious to him that this girl was exactly that: a girl. She could be no older than fifteen years old. He stared into her dead eyes. Now, Monks knew that he was violent, nasty and often sex-obsessed, but when it came to certain deeds he also had some ethics. He felt pity for this tiny girl.

'Why are you here so late at night? Go home to your mother.'

Her glazed eyes stared up at him. 'You want some business, mister?' she repeated, as if on autopilot. Monks took fifty dollars from his wallet and handed it over to her, then said, 'Go home to your mother, sweetheart. You shouldn't be here, it's too dangerous.' With that, he kissed her on the cheek, and then went to the youth hostel, angry that anyone's mother could let a young child drift into such a depraved lifestyle.

10

All on Top

England

The morning after the night before – sometimes it's a good one, often a bad one. This was a good one. When Luke woke up, Shannon had gone into the kitchen to make coffee. Rubbing the sleep out of his eyes, he grinned as he remembered the wild sex they'd had last night. Shannon came into the bedroom with two cups. She looked stunning, even first thing in the morning. Result, I've pulled a diamond here, he thought.

'Sleep well?' asked Shannon.

'Yeah, like a log.'

'Last night was great,' she said.

Luke felt embarrassed at that remark. All he could think to say was, 'Thank you.'

Shannon roared with laughter. 'You're not supposed to say thank you!'

She almost knocked the cups of coffee over as she rolled over on the bed, still laughing hard. Luke put his head in his hands. 'I know, what a twat.' He could feel his face burning, and he started chuckling away. She moved in close to him. They were giggling like children. Then she whispered into his ear, 'How about making me want to thank you some more?' Luke did not need much persuading as he'd had a hard-on as soon as she had walked back in with the coffees. In seconds, they began frantically making love as passionately as if they had not stopped all night.

That evening, Luke met up with Monks in their local pub.

'What are we going to do about our problem?' Monks asked.

'Well, I guess we have to involve him.'

'Fuck him,' Monks said.

'How are we going to do that?'

'Kill the fucker.'

Luke laughed. 'You are joking.'

He was not. 'No, let's do him in.'

Luke soon realised that Monks was serious. 'Listen, mate, let's just give him a one-off payment then disappear for a while.'

'I'm not running away, Luke.'

Luke knew that Monks was scared of nothing and nobody, but this was all too heavy for him. He had been in a few ruckuses and tight spots with him over the years and knew that he was probably not far off insane. He could see in Monks' eyes that he wanted to kill a top man. Luke may have been a bit of a rogue from time to time, but murder? He certainly did not want to find himself caught up in anything like that.

'I love you man, you know that,' he told Monks.

'I know. Luke, this cunt will never stop bothering us.'

'Monks, I'm not a killer.'

'I'll do it; I just need your back-up.'

Luke couldn't believe what his friend was asking him to do.

'They'll know it's us.'

'How? He has loads of enemies – we're doing someone a favour.'

Luke would never let his friend down, so reluctantly he

asked Monks what he had planned and, more importantly, how they were going to get away with it.

'I've worked it all out – it's foolproof.'

Monks switched off his phone so they wouldn't be disturbed. Luke sighed, wishing he were with Shannon, far away from here. Monks looked around and then proceeded to explain his foolproof plan.

Tuesday evening, Luke took a call from Shannon as he was closing the shop. 'Okay, I'll come over at seven, see you later,' he said. She somehow sounded different on the phone, as if she were worried about something or other. He said to himself that it was probably nothing and then finished locking the security grill on the shop. Luke then phoned Monks to make sure that he was still on for the following night. 'No problem, Luke, it's all set up,' his friend assured him.

Luke took the Tube from west to south of the river. He knocked on the door of Shannon's small flat. They hadn't known each other all that long – well, barely a week. As she answered the door, Luke could feel his heart pounding like a jackrabbit's. 'Hi babes, come in,' she said. Shannon was dressed in a pair of tight jeans and a loose fitting top. Luke admired her body. She could wear sackcloth and she would still manage to look gorgeous, Luke thought as he followed her into the flat. They kissed as they sat down on the sofa. Shannon knew she would have to tell him her important news sooner rather than later. Luke had already sussed out that something was wrong: could she be bored of him already? What had he done to put her off him?

'Luke, we need to talk,' she began.

Here we go, she's dumping me, he thought. 'I knew it, I could tell on the phone.' He could feel his stomach sinking and looked away from her.

'No, Luke, please pay attention to all I have to say.'

She seemed quite upset. He prepared for the bad news.

'I'm leaving London on Saturday, I have to go home.'

Luke heard what she had said but felt confused.

'Why? We've only just started seeing each other.'

She held onto his hand. 'No, you don't understand.'

She was right. He didn't. It had been all over the news that a man had nearly bled to death with his penis in his hands while another had had his head caved in with a tripod. The police were treating it as a strange ritualistic attempted double murder. Of course, Shannon had no idea whether they could trace this back to her, but she certainly didn't need to take that risk. She couldn't possibly tell him the reason why she had to move on, but she didn't want to lose him so soon after meeting him.

In the short time Luke had known her, he had thought that this was the real thing. Or could it just be infatuation? He took this on board then stood up, ready to leave.

'Right then, I suppose I had better go.'

'Don't be like that,' she pleaded, clearly upset with his reaction.

'Well, what do you expect –'

Before he could finish she interrupted and asked him to sit down and let her finish telling him why she had asked him over here. Luke responded by sitting on the sofa to hear her out.

'All right, I'm listening.'

Shannon knelt down beside him, held his hand and gazed lovingly into his eyes as she made her proposition to him.

'I know this sounds crazy…' She paused.

'Go on.' Luke's heart raced.

'Come with me.' Yes, he thought, he knew that they had a connection. Hang on a minute, though – Australia? This weekend? That didn't give him much time, it was all a bit sudden. 'SHIT!' he shouted out loud. This was not what he had expected. I cannot leave everything behind by the weekend, he thought. His mind was blurred. What about the shop, his phone swindle and all the easy cash he was making with Monks, his mum and brother – they needed him. This was all happening too fast.

'When do you say, on Saturday?'

'Yes, babes, you and me in Sydney.'

He thought about the madness of it all. Then it hit home – what an escape route! He had stashed away a small fortune from the trips around the country picking up phones. Maybe he could avoid all the upcoming bullshit with Danny Chilton and the mob. This could be perfect, he thought. Then he switched back to the real world. How would he obtain a visa for Australia in less than a week? And with his criminal record they wouldn't let him in, would they?

Shannon babbled on excitedly about rolling around in the surf, the sunny days, just the two of them – it would be great, she explained. He agreed it was a lovely thought, living in the sun. He had never really considered moving overseas. He was a West London boy at heart and he liked it that way.

'I want to, I really do, but by Saturday …'

'I know it's short notice, but come on, seize the moment.'

Shannon began rubbing his thigh. She was buzzing with exhilaration. Trying to ignore the hard-on she had now caused, Luke's head was swimming with a mix of 'Can I go? Should I stay?' What a dilemma he had found himself in.

'Life's too short, babes, let's not waste a second.'

She was right, he knew that much. 'I want to, but this weekend's too soon.'

Feeling bitterly disappointed, Shannon asked him why he didn't want to go with her. He would love to, he did not want to let her down, but he had to think what he should do for the best.

'I do, but I can't just up and leave on a whim.'

She smiled and carried on rubbing his inner thigh. She thought she would leave it for now as her desire for him grew. She wanted him physically right then; he turned her on so much it hurt. So she made a suggestion which she knew he would like. 'Let's go to bed.'

Luke did not hesitate at her splendid idea, and they moved into the bedroom so they could make love. They seemed to have decided that they would discuss this quandary once again in the morning.

Uncle Darren was worried. One of Danny Chilton's mob had just popped in to give him a reminder that they would be visiting shortly to confirm their up-and-coming business arrangement. Seeing as Darren could not figure out what the hell he was talking about, he nervously smiled and replied, 'Yes, okay.' He presumed it would be concerning one of his nephew's sidelines, which he knew were not always strictly legitimate.

An hour later, Luke arrived for work. Darren offered to make a brew.

'That would be spot on, thanks,' said Luke.

'Everything all right, Luke?'

'Yeah, fine, are you?'

Darren had to find out what he had been playing at. 'Why is Danny Chilton sniffing around here then?'

Luke had been dreading his uncle getting caught up in all of this.

'I'm so sorry, Darren, it's been unavoidable.'

Darren came out of the kitchen with the tea. 'I've warned you about him: steer clear.'

'I know, we're going to sort it.'

'What do you mean?' asked Darren.

'It is going to be sound, don't worry.'

Uncle Darren had a worried look on his face. He moved in close to his nephew. 'I know you duck and dive a little, but you have to be careful.'

'Honest, it's all under control,' Luke assured him.

Darren sighed. He realised it was best not to ask too much

more. He cared so much for his nephew, but there would be very little he could do if he would be dealing with these gangsters. 'Luke, think how this may affect your family. They don't need the hassle.'

Luke was well aware of their safety; that was his main concern. However, Monks had a plan, and even though he was not keen they would have to see it through.

Thursday, about dusk, Luke met up with his accomplice. They had everything worked out, but it had to run like clockwork. Luke still had not sussed whether Monks was serious or not. He hoped that they were just going to try to strike a deal with the man, and that he would be so impressed with their bottle that they would become valuable members of the team. Was this a wise move? Now was the time to find out.

Monks had done his homework. He had been watching Danny's movements for quite some time now. The man he had been talking to about shifting a bit of gear had unintentionally given him some useful information about Danny Chilton's empire. The rumours about this villain were that at least two minders always surrounded him at any given time. He never held any interest in female company, unlike his brother Jack, who couldn't get enough of the opposite sex. This inevitably led to rumours that Danny must be gay. It was also partly because there were always men with him, though that was purely for his own security. The truth of it was that Danny Chilton was interested in neither men nor women; he was one hundred percent asexual. His only lust was for money, pure and simple. The only time he was alone was between six to six-forty-five in the evening. That was the period when he spent valuable time walking his two treasured Alsatians in the park.

Monks was once again explaining to Luke the procedure that would keep Danny off their case forever.

'You understand me?' he asked Luke.

Luke nodded. He hoped that it would all go smoothly. They took up their position near to the park exit. Nobody was around, which was perfectly normal, as people tended to stay away from parks in the autumn once it started to go dark. They could become dangerous environments. It seemed strange that a security conscious villain such as Danny Chilton always left three quarters of an hour in his day when he would be completely vulnerable. Perhaps he presumed that with two mean-looking animals with him no potential enemy would dare to come anywhere near, for fear of the beasts tearing them to shreds.

While they waited, Luke let scenarios run through his mind: they would give him the opportunity to change his view on their operation, and then he would congratulate them on their sheer courage in confronting him, thus proving themselves as worthy adversaries and joining his team of gangsters and making a small fortune as his two main players. What was he doing here? Why had he let Monks talk him into this? Luke did not like the fact that the local gangster had decided to tax them for their inventiveness, but surely after a couple of payments he would lose interest and leave them alone? Christ, that's too far-fetched, he thought – he's never going to go for that in a million years. Stick to the plan, it'll be fine, he told himself.

'It's past six,' he said to Monks.

'I know, just hang on.'

They could make out a figure in the distance. As Luke watched the figure move closer towards them, he could see a large dog on each side, straining at its leash. Luke took deep, slow breaths as Danny Chilton strode ever nearer.

'Right, get ready.'

Luke realised that the moment of truth was near and tried to remain calm. He uneasily placed his hand onto the large blade inside his pocket. Monks was itching to get the job done. He turned and gave Luke the nod. Luke stepped out in front of Danny.

'Hello, Mr Chilton.'

Danny stopped abruptly.

'I didn't know you lived here, son.'

Luke hated it when he called him son. He anxiously grasped the knife, prepared to strike if needed.

'I don't,' he said.

Danny took a step back. Instinct told him he could be in a spot of bother. Monks appeared in a flash. In one action the machete in his hand came down and almost severed the head clean off the shoulders of one of the dogs. Danny immediately let go of the other Alsatian, which went for Monks, jumping straight up at him. Danny turned and began to run back towards his home. Monks was knocked to the ground by the force of the Alsatian. Luckily for him, before it could sink its teeth into his neck he managed to slice open the canine's stomach. Silently, the mutt lay still on top of him, bleeding profusely. He pushed the carcass off.

'Fuck, go after him!' he ordered Luke.

Following hastily, Luke caught up with Danny in five strides. He tackled Danny rugby style to the wet grass. Monks was now in pursuit, covered in the blood of the second dog that he had killed.

Wrestling on the damp surface, Danny, who was certainly no mug, manoeuvred around to find himself on top of Luke. He punched Luke twice in succession, the first one glancing off the crown of his head but the second one connecting with his right eye socket. Luke felt it sting sharply. Monks had arrived just in time and aimed a brutal kick at the back of Danny's head. Danny scrambled to his feet, spinning away from another kick. Luke grabbed the knife from his pocket, rose halfway to his feet then swiped it around, catching Danny across his solar plexus. With a natural instinct Danny grabbed onto his side. 'You fucking ...'

Monks helped Luke to his feet. 'You're going to die,' he said. He slashed Danny at an angle, cutting half his ear off. As Danny staggered to the left, Luke plunged the knife back into his stomach before twisting it in for maximum effect. Danny held onto Luke with an almighty grip.

'You'd better fucking finish the job, son,' he spluttered, blood and spit dripping from his mouth.

'Don't call me son,' Luke answered.

Danny did not cry out or wince in pain. He just kept holding on, staring into Luke's eyes. He tried to speak but could say no more. He just stared until he let go and fell to the ground. Luke stood there with the bloodstained knife in his hand, in shock at what he had just done. Monks pushed Danny over with his right foot.

'He's dead, thank god.' He put his arm on Luke's shoulder. 'You did him.'

Luke dropped the knife. Monks picked it back up then took a bag from his jacket and simply put the tools they had used into it. Tapping Luke on the back he said, 'We have to skip, mate.'

A cold wind blew through the empty park. 'Come on, Luke, we can't stay here.'

'Yeah, I'm coming.'

They looked around; there was nobody in sight. It had gone like a dream as far as Monks was concerned. Luke did not feel the same. They swiftly walked out of the park, both of them covered in thick red blood. They quickly got to Luke's car. Not a soul had seen them enter or leave the park. Monks took Luke's keys.

'I'll drive to the shop, we have to get rid of all this.'

'Yeah, you better,' was all Luke could manage to say.

Monks started the engine and pulled away as calmly as if nothing had happened at all.

11

Milo and Harwood

Sydney

Kerry Symonds had stayed at her brother Paul's bedside for
almost week and he had still not come around. There was
only the two of them left in their family, apart from a distant
aunt who lived somewhere down in South Australia. Losing
both their parents when they were quite young had had an
effect on the pair. It had always been tough for them, but
they had always stuck together and taken good care of each
other since then. Now Kerry, a good Catholic girl, was
praying that her younger brother would pull out of his coma
as soon as possible. Her brother looked as if he was sleeping.
His face had more or less returned to normal – most of the
horrific swelling had gone down.

Dr Robb was concerned. He came in to speak to Kerry as
he did on a daily basis.

'Hello, Miss Symonds, how are you today?' Stupid
question, he thought as soon as he said it.

'Not had much sleep, how do you think I am doing?' she
replied curtly.

Fair enough, he thought. 'Well, there is still no change in
your brother's condition. I am afraid we may have to
consider the options we discussed yesterday once more.'

'I'm sorry, doctor, but the Lord gives and the Lord takes

away. I do not wish to disobey the scriptures; only He will decide my poor brother's destiny.'

To which Dr Robb replied, 'I fully appreciate your strongly held beliefs, Miss Symonds, but as we explained to you, even if your brother does come out of this coma he will not be able to do anything, or live any type of normal life. He will not move from this hospital bed. Effectively, he will be a vegetable. Miss Symonds, there is no more we can do for him. I implore you – the kindest thing you can do for your brother is to switch off the ventilator.'

'No, I've told you, I cannot do this. I do not have the right, it is in God's hands.'

She then held her brother's limp arm, and began to pray yet again. Dr Robb, a compassionate man, placed a tender hand on Kerry's shoulder for a second, and then he left them in peace in the room.

Kerry prayed for forgiveness. She knew her brother was no angel. Why was God punishing them? She begged the Lord to give her brother one more chance. She promised that she would watch him, protect him and keep him away from all the destructive influences and temptations that he had followed before. Give him the opportunity to prove that he has a good and kindly spirit, she prayed. Let me help him, please Lord. Kerry stopped praying and started to cry, wondering why life had treated her so badly.

Milo had had the week off work since the fight at The Hero of Waterloo. He had taken the nurse he chatted up, whose name was Lisa, out on a date and felt he should be getting some return for his efforts. Being a cultured, or so he thought, sophisticated fellow, on the second date Milo was wining and dining the young nurse at the restaurant Forty-One. This offered the most impressive vistas of Sydney Harbour and a fine French menu with plenty of Asian influence. He thought to himself that if this place did not close the deal tonight, the little prick tease may have to be taught a lesson. The thought of this prospect excited him; sometimes he enjoyed forcing disobedient little tarts to do his will. He stopped himself thinking that way; she may yet comply with what he had on offer later. Because you never know, with some of them, they like it that way. However, not all of them – then it can become awkward. After all, he had enough experience of it.

Milo turned on all of his best charm to keep her at ease. He ordered the waiter to bring them another bottle of Shiraz (Hermitage) straight from the Barossa Valley. Lisa was distinctly impressed with his vast knowledge of all the Australian vineyards. She had fallen for all his well-rehearsed patter, which he had used on many previous occasions, usually with a great deal of success. Milo could read all the signs. He could tell that this one was in the bag. Still, back to work tomorrow, he mused. As she could well be willing, he might not have to waste any time destroying or covering his tracks. The waiter presented the fresh bottle and charged their glasses.

'That was a lovely meal,' Lisa enthused. 'I'm not used to such delightful restaurants, you know.'

'Really? I'm glad you're enjoying it here.'

'I've only got a few months left until I'm qualified. This is all a bit too expensive on student nurse wages,' she explained.

'Stick with me, and this sort of thing could be a pretty regular occurrence.'

She was now even more overwhelmed. All Milo could think of now was getting her out of here and back to his house to have his way with her.

'I really cannot eat another thing,' Lisa said, sitting back in her chair. 'That was more than anyone can eat.'

'Are you sure? They do a delicious dessert carte du jour.'

Milo was pleased with himself for adding a touch of French

for effect, and even more contented that she wanted no more food, as he felt he had spent enough money tonight. He immediately asked for the bill, and then he smiled at her reassuringly. They both lifted their glasses at the same time and drank some more wine.

Harwood slumped into his chair in the canteen, placing the small plastic tray loaded up with two pork kebabs on skewers with special fried rice on the table. He pushed the rice around his plate aimlessly. He didn't know why he had piled his plate high with food, as he was not particularly hungry. He had just finished a crap afternoon shift and was in a foul mood. He hated working without his regular partner, Milo. He could hear the conversation of a couple of rookie cops discussing their day's events; he wanted to tell them to shut the fuck up. He had a nasty migraine coming on and listening to two not-been-on-the-job-for-more-than-a-week newbies going on excitedly about some shitty small-time dealer they had managed to arrest earlier today was not helping him very much.

Just then Milo came in and sat down next to him.

'How are you, Aaron? Missing me this week, are you?' he jibed. He slapped his coffee down on the bench. Milo looked refreshed and rested, and was acting as if he were full of all the joys of spring. Unfortunately, Harwood was feeling completely the opposite of the rather chipper-looking Milo.

'I've had a rotten day, mate. I had to babysit a useless newbie. I swear they get more stupid every year, you know.' He made sure he said this loud enough for the two newcomers to hear him. They both looked round at him, then quickly turned away when they saw who had made that barbed comment. Milo laughed out approvingly as the two rookies carried on their conversation, only in a rather more hushed tone.

'Anyway, mate, are you still set for tonight?' Milo asked.

'Wouldn't want to miss it for anything. What time is the meet again?'

'I'll pick you up at nine-thirty – make sure you're ready.'

'Definitely, I'll be fighting fit and raring to go,' he replied. Still, he couldn't help wondering why Milo seemed so full of beans this afternoon.

Aaron Harwood and Nathan 'Milo' Mills had been partners in the New South Wales police department for over seven years give or take a month or so. They had a good mutual understanding. For well beyond six of those years they had become the two most corrupt, dishonest police officers ever to grace the uniform of New South Wales' finest. They would take backhanders from just about any felon they could find. Between them, after a hell of a lot of research, they probably knew and had dealings with every minor drug dealer, pimp, prostitute, thief, or any other unscrupulous rogue with little or no morals at all. Every detail was written down and catalogued in their little black book of all the scumbags of New South Wales and its proximity.

It never started out that way. Aaron James Harwood was born the third child of a hard-working, second-generation Scottish immigrant family of farmers that had settled near Hobart in Tasmania. He was destined to carry on the success-ful dairy farm business his grandfather had begun fifty years ago. It would have given him a decent living. But growing up in rural Tasmania was never going to be good enough for Harwood. He wanted to get away from Tasmania from the age of around fifteen years old; it was far too dull for him. He had always fancied being a police officer in the city as it seemed an exciting alternative to life on a farm in the middle of nowhere.

As for his friend Milo, he was a completely different kettle of fish, hailing from a wealthy, prominent Western Australian background. He had no real reason to deal in the murky world of deceit and corruption, he just enjoyed the danger of it all and he liked the power it gave him.

Scratching his thick ginger goatee beard, Harwood pushed his plate away. Milo picked at the pork kebabs. He couldn't even stop himself from eating somebody else's food, which summed up his greedy nature. If it was there, Milo had to take it. He believed that everything was owed to him, even half-eaten kebabs. Stuffing his mouth full, Milo explained what the job would be later that day.

'After I pick you up we can catch the little shit on his way to the club.'

'Should I be tooled up?' asked Harwood.

'Yes, mate, it'll shake him up a bit. He won't be any bother, I know that for a fact.'

'You'd better be right; we don't need it getting messy like the last number,' Harwood said, giving Milo a concerned look.

'Chill out, mate – that was a one-off. This job is a piece of cake, I promise. Nothing can go wrong.'

With that Milo stood up and grabbed the last of the meat off Harwood's plate. He looked across at the two rookies, who were still sitting down muttering to each other, then said to Harwood, 'Just look at those useless pair of cunts. They are going fucking nowhere. To think we were like that once. What a waste of fucking space. Have you finished your shift? Let's take a walk, mate.'

Harwood glanced over at them, seeing how young and naive they looked, grinned at Milo, then stood up and left the canteen with his partner in crime. He felt slightly melancholy as he thought about his first year in the job, before he became mixed up with the easy money, easy girls and all the trappings that had started coming his way once he came to realise how much a little gentle persuasion and turning a blind eye occasionally can benefit a police officer on the beat.

Harwood and Milo passed by the reception area on their way out of the police station. As they neared the exit, the grizzly old custody sergeant, McCabe, who seemed to be constantly suspicious of them, called them both back for a quick word.

'I've had another complaint about you two pair of bastards,' he said.

Harwood looked stunned at this accusation. 'Surely we are not being accused of anything, Sergeant McCabe?'

McCabe interrupted. 'Don't play the innocent with me. I have been in this job a long time. I am watching you two very closely, so be warned. Cool it with the prisoners when you pull them in, okay?'

Presuming that McCabe could not touch them, they both nodded at the sergeant. 'No worries, Sergeant McCabe,' they answered in unison.

McCabe was a wily old-school copper. He did not like those two. He had seen it all before: good police officers, bad police officers. A niggling sense was always pulling at him about their activities. McCabe was sure they were up to no good. Bent coppers – they were no good to anyone. Milo was the one he could not bear. He was as corrupt as they come. But though he was absolutely convinced Milo was bad to the bone, he had a gut feeling that Harwood was not in the same mould. He was positive that there was a good copper in him – he would just have to get him away from his partner. You had to give him credit – Sergeant McCabe had a nose for these things, and he had never been wrong yet. He and all hard-working police officers despised officers on the take. He desperately wanted to nail them but he would need watertight evidence. Of course, that would take a lot of painstaking effort, and would be a hell of a lot easier said than done. They will slip up, he thought, and when they did McCabe was determined to be there to see it. He grumbled an unintelligible retort at them as they left the station to make their way home.

*   *   *

Harwood opened the porch door of his ramshackle three-bedroom house situated in the suburb of Epping, 18 kilometres north of Sydney in the City of Parramatta. He had only rented it twelve months ago in what was an affluent area. Not that it made any difference to Harwood, for even after such a short period his home looked totally out of character with the smart, tidy homes that surrounded his. There could be no doubt that the place was in need of a woman's touch. The furniture was tatty; the scuffed wooden floors needed resurfacing. The kitchen was dirty, the cabinets were ancient – they almost certainly had been there thirty years ago or more. The refrigerator was only a year old, it was the only recent addition to the house. He gazed out of his front window and thought that he must clean the garden up soon, as the grass was nearly a foot long and was a real eyesore compared with perfectly manicured lawns in the rest of the street. Harwood was comfortable with this as it meant none of the neighbours ever hassled him or would even suspect that he was a police officer, and that suited him just fine.

Unkempt as it was, Harwood knew his house would be a safe haven. He figured the untidy appearance may be enough to give the outside world the impression that the man who lived there was your typical, hardy little Aussie battler, who against all the odds kept on grafting away, paying his taxes, with not a lot left to show for it after that. Perhaps your average criminal would not look twice at Harwood's dishevelled-looking house, choosing instead one of his neighbour's tidy, pristine homes to break in to, not knowing that hidden in Harwood's residence was over $150,000 and in all probability enough narcotics to supply half of Sydney's drug addicts for six months or more. He went to freshen up before getting some rest until he had to pick up the required merchandise.

Meanwhile, Milo was busy planning the next month's appointments, flicking through the little black book, marking down certain clients on whom they had not leaned for a while. He frowned as he read out the name Andy Karacan. Unfortunately, he had to delete this member off his list, as Andy Karacan had become a liability. Although a good earner for them, he seemed rather loose with his tongue in particular company. It had all got out of hand, and not for the first time Milo and Harwood had had to deal with the matter, quickly and efficiently. At the back of his book was a special section noting how many times they had had to carry out these necessary tasks. He took a great deal of satisfaction from the fact that they never let these situations drag on for very long. But seeing as they had taken these measures four times now, it was becoming a concern.

12

How Did He Get Involved?

England

Luke sat outside his mother's house in his car. He watched for any movement inside, waiting for all of the lights to go out before he would contemplate sneaking in so that he could try to sleep. He had already been back to Monks' place to spend time with the accomplice who had helped him commit murder. They had both showered, changed and burnt all their clothes in the chimenea out in the back garden, getting rid of all the evidence that could link them to the crime. All of the blood that had soaked through to their skin had now disappeared up in smoke. Monks had promised to take care of what remained – the tools that were used to kill Danny Chilton. He texted Luke telling him not to worry; nothing could tie them to the demise of Danny. Luke was yet to be convinced; he did not feel as laid-back about the whole scenario. How can Monks be so nonplussed by it all? he thought. The last light went out indoors. Luke decided to give it ten minutes before getting out of his car.

Old Mr Kravis was still up, looking out of his window across the way. He could see Luke sitting in his car. Mr Kravis was so fond of all the Crooks family; they had always treated him kindly. His granddaughter had grown up with Luke. They went to primary and secondary school together and they were very close for a long time. He knew that Luke could be a bit of a rogue, but he liked him – he could see that he had a good heart. However, Mr Kravis had a nose for trouble. It might have been his natural instinct, but he could tell when danger was near. After all, these were the same instincts that helped him during World War Two; they seemed to kick in like a type of sixth sense. He had felt perturbed since he had noticed a couple of Danny Chilton's heavies nosing around, looking at the Crooks' household at different times of the day and night recently. Mr Kravis was a wily old fox, very observant. He knew Luke mixed with a few dodgy people occasionally, and so he liked to keep an eye on who was knocking around the neighbourhood.

Luke moved from his car to step indoors. He glimpsed a sight of Mr Kravis as he looked across to the dimly lit front room of his council property. The curtains twitched as Mr Kravis moved away from the window, trying not to look like he was interfering. Luke waved at the window; he did not mind if the old man was watching the world go by at night. He was well aware that the old man liked to observe to see that his neighbours were all safe and secure at home. It was quite chilly for an October evening, especially at this hour. Luke walked to the front door. Taking out his keys he slowly unlocked the latch, then gently closed the door behind him. Heading for the kitchen with an incredible thirst, he raided the fridge to drink some ice-cold milk. Quietly, Luke went up the stairs, not wanting to wake anyone. He did not want to speak to another soul, at least until the morning. Creeping into his room, he fumbled towards the bed, kicked off his shoes, then lay perfectly still as he thought of what had transpired. He so wanted to be with Shannon right now, she would make him feel better about the dreadful crime that he and Monks had committed. He felt worn out; all his strength had drained out of him. He closed his eyes and convinced himself that it would all turn out for the best and within five minutes he fell into a long, deep sleep.

It did not take long for the police to close off the murder scene. Both of Danny Chilton's top minders had arrived at the park and were in conversation with two senior CID officers. The forensic team had turned up and had erected a large white canvas tent to help preserve any evidence. There were lots of flashing lights and uniformed police all rushing around looking busy. Danny's corpse lay face down on the wet grass, covered in blood. Two Alsatians lay slaughtered near his body. It was a truly horrendous scene, although the CID officers were not so surprised once they had found out who the victim of the attack was.

'He always walks the dogs at this time,' said Danny's co-driver Pug, clearly stunned that anyone in the parish would have dared to kill the main man.

'Thanks, we'll be in touch.' The CID officer knew Danny was a nasty piece of work. Nevertheless, he still had to do his duty. Rixon and Pug were now free to leave the scene, as it was obvious that they worked for the victim and would have nothing to gain by disposing of their boss. In fact, they would be in it up to their necks once Jack Chilton found out that his brother was dead. Given that the two of them were unable to prevent this happening on their watch, the future did not look too bright for either of them.

13

Dodgy Dealer Redfern Way

Sydney

Luke woke up early – it was something like seven-thirty. He had always been a light sleeper and it never took much to wake him up, unlike Shannon – she was still dead to the world. Luke did not mind, as he liked to watch her sleep. She looked beautiful as she lay there, not moving a muscle. He grinned like a child, thinking to himself how the sex they'd had last night had, as usual, been mind-blowing. Those two had a natural way of making each other feel good. They just clicked, and they continued to do so, even though they were now living in each other's pockets. Luke sat up next to her, slowly moving to get out of bed. He gently kissed Shannon, trying not to wake her. He went out of the bedroom and down the stairs to the kitchen to make a light breakfast for them both. In anticipation of spending an enjoyable, quiet morning at home with Shannon he decided he would not call Monks as he gazed out across at Manly Quay. It was now a week since the incident at The Hero of Waterloo and he had no real desire to be reminded of those events by his old friend.

Shannon awoke as Luke put the mug of hot coffee next to her on the bedside cabinet. He sat beside her with her favourite breakfast: lightly toasted English muffins with butter and strawberry preserve. A classic way to start the day, he thought.

'Thank you, honey, what have I done to deserve this?'

'It's Sunday morning, sweetheart – I thought I would treat you. Let's spend a day at the beach.'

'Sure thing, that's what a Sunday is made for.'

She reached across to kiss him; they were ready to get it on. As Luke returned the embrace, the phone started ringing. Should he answer it? After all, he knew who it would be on the other end of the line. Luke went to go and get the call but Shannon pulled him back towards her.

'Leave it for now, stay here in bed with me. You can return the call later on, honey.'

Caught up in the moment, Luke agreed this was a good idea. Monks, or whoever dared to call at this time on a perfect Sunday morning, would just have to wait as his hands were now cupping that oh-so-succulent ass once more.

When they re-emerged from bed sometime later, it didn't take Luke five minutes to get dressed for the beach. He threw on a pair of khaki three-quarter-length Levis cargo pants and a loose-fitting Lyle and Scott pale-blue polo shirt, completing the look with a pair of stylish green Brazilian Havaianas flip-flops on his feet.

'Wait up, I'm not ready yet,' Shannon cried out.

'I'm not going anywhere without you, Shannon, I'll sit out here on the balcony until you're fit to go.' Why do women take so long to get ready? he thought. We're only walking thirty paces to chill out on the sand for the morning. Still, he didn't really mind – she would look stunning lying next to him, and all the surfer dudes would be giving her admiring glances. He loved the fact that she was so sexy, and he couldn't help enjoying the attention she got from strangers, knowing that she only had eyes for him. All the blokes must look at him thinking: 'You lucky bastard, that girl of yours is fucking gorgeous.'

She eventually came out onto the veranda in a floppy sun hat, a purple sarong and a matching string bikini top, carrying with her a tiny moccasin-style clutch bag.

'Come on, honey, I want to catch the best of the sun before it gets too hot.'

'Absolutely, babes, let's get down there.'

He watched as she turned around, approving of the fine ensemble she had chosen.

From their penthouse apartment it was only a few short steps to the elevator. Luke pressed the button for the lift and its doors opened immediately. That is the advantage of having the best property in the building – first-class service. And so it should be – it had cost Shannon enough money for the privilege. Of course, this was something else Luke adored about his princess: she had money, and plenty of it. Monks was constantly reminding him of that particular fact and how he should take full advantage of it. Luke agreed with him to a certain point, but he would never dream of taking the piss. He enjoyed a few bonuses, but didn't like the thought of being a kept man, so he liked to earn his own few quid to contribute. Her wealth was cool, though, when he was short.

Stepping out of the elevator, he nodded to another random door attendant he didn't recognise. The sun was searing hot for half past ten in the morning, knocking them back as they left the air-conditioned building. As they strolled over to the beach they simultaneously put on their Ray-Ban sunglasses, laughing at the motion. Luke held Shannon's hand. Manly Beach was crowded and this often gave the place a real good vibe on a weekend. All the day-trippers, tourists and a smattering of locals seemed to have converged down on Manly Beach today. They decide to amble along the water's edge towards the promenade, until coming across a quieter part of the beach. They settled down in close proximity to the lively pedestrianised plaza called The Corso, which by this time of day was always a non-stop hive of activity.

This main thoroughfare of souvenir shops and fast food outlets was surrounded by the constant buzz Manly seemed to hold, full of sunbathers looking to catch plenty of rays. Life is feeling very good today, Luke thought as he stretched out on the warm sand next to Shannon. They sat just close enough to the ocean that the water lapped up at their feet.

Meanwhile, over the harbour in the inner-city suburb of Redfern, Harwood and Milo were in confrontation with one of their 'associates' who owed them money. Harwood always seemed to be angry these days. He realised straight away that they had let this one spin out of control. 'No worries,' Milo had said, once again. Maybe it was time to stop dealing with these unstable, unpredictable junkies. The fact was he really did not want to have to dispose of another scumbag.

'Stop fucking crying, you prick, it isn't going to make any difference so shut the fuck up,' Milo shouted at the scruffy dealer. He had completely lost it. The pair of them seemed to be continually swinging from one mood to another. Harwood shifted between angry and trying to remain calm. Standing in the dealer's bathroom, he watched him beg for his life. He had seen that look on Milo's face before – the expression of a man who was beginning to lose his sense of reality. Harwood had secured all the doors to the grubby, unkempt flat and was now preparing to do some damage. The dealer asked for another week to come up with the money.

'Please man, I will have all the cash for you by next Friday, I promise,' he pleaded.

'Listen, I am going to ask you one more time, and if I do not get the answer we are looking for, you are going to die. Is that understood?' Milo yelled.

The scruffy dealer was now terrified. He began to shake uncontrollably as Harwood aimed his colt .380 at his head.

'Now then, let's start again. Where's the ten grand you robbed from Andy Karacan a month ago?'

'I told you, Milo, it is all gone. I cannot get hold of any more cash until next week,' the dealer babbled. 'Why do you two not believe me?'

'Because you're an oily little bastard, that's why. I'm very fucking bored of this now, so produce the goods.'

'Please, there is no money.'

Milo cracked his knuckles and then smiled at the hapless dealer.

'Hold on a minute.' Harwood intervened just as Milo had arranged a knuckleduster onto his right fist.

'What's wrong with you?' Milo asked, without really expecting Harwood to offer any type of answer.

'He's telling the truth, mate,' said Harwood, who was now feeling more calm and relaxed. The dealer obviously didn't have any money – he would have handed some over by now if he had any stashed away.

'I don't believe the scumbag, he's holding out on us,' said Milo, who wasn't having any of it.

'Listen to him, man – it's all gone, I swear to you,' the scruffy dealer said as he went down onto his knees, begging for mercy. Harwood's attitude remained mellow; he even began to soften towards the dealer and feel some sympathy for the useless excuse of a man cowering and quivering in front of them. Regrettably for the scruffy dealer, Milo had no such compassion. This man was lying to them, and he wasn't going to stand for it.

'You've had your crack at it, now it's time to pay the price,' he menaced. He slowly lifted his right arm and in one swift movement hit the dealer with a powerful blow. The scruffy dealer fell to the ground, cracking his skull hard on the tacky linoleum floor.

'Shit, Milo, he doesn't have anything. Isn't it fucking obvious?'

The scruffy dealer twitched nervously as he started to regain consciousness. Looking slightly disorientated he touched the side of his face, which had swelled up to the size of a small orange. Knowing that he was now in serious trouble, he was trying to think where he could find some money quickly to try to appease Milo, who stared down at him waiting for some information. He could tell that Milo would not take no for an answer for much longer.

'Okay, I can get you a load of gear right now, but you will have to come over there with me – it's a bit of a distance away, though.'

Harwood was not too sure if this would be a good move right at this moment. However, Milo wanted a score. Harwood was not feeling too positive about what the scruffy dealer was suggesting to them.

The scruffy dealer looked up at Milo's sneering face. Milo reached down and grabbed the scruffy dealer by the lapels of his tatty jacket and pulled him up until their faces were an inch or so apart. Staring directly into the scruffy dealer's petrified eyes, Milo could tell that he was now in such a state of fear and panic that he was clearly desperate to do whatever it would take to get these two psychotic cops off his case.

'Okay, here is what's going to happen now. I am going to ask one more question. All you are going to do is tell me the correct answer. Then we shall go to the destination you give me and collect the readies – is that simple enough for you?'

'Whatever you say,' agreed the dealer. Then, before he had the chance to say any more, Milo spun him around and hit him a severe blow on the other side of his face, sending him crashing onto the linoleum floor once again.

'I have not asked the relevant question yet. Now, I will start again.'

Milo had just wanted to hit the dealer again to see if his serrated knuckleduster could really do the business. The other side of the dealer's face swelled up, giving him the strange appearance of having a tennis-ball-sized lump on each side of his head. Milo opened his fist, impressed by what the medieval-shaped implement had embossed onto the man's face.

Harwood helped the battered dealer up onto his knees. Wobbling around a bit, he looked up at Milo, not daring to say another word.

'Good, I think you finally understand. Now, where can we go to get that ten grand?'

The scruffy dealer composed himself. 'Mount Druitt,' he said. 'We have a connection out there. It's a clubhouse and they're heavy blokes, mind.'

Milo scratched his chin and looked at Harwood. 'What do you reckon, mate?'

Harwood glanced at the dealer's face. The dealer was in a no-win situation, he thought. Could he just be trying to create a diversion? As he thought about what they should do, Harwood remembered that he'd once had dealings somewhere out that very way. He was positive that the address the scruffy dealer was talking about was a biker gang clubhouse, and that he was either in with an outlaw motorcycle gang or he owed them a debt. He may well be hedging his bets by taking a couple of corrupt police officers to their clubhouse, knowing that the gang's record with the New South Wales Police was not what you would call harmonious.

'Get yourself cleaned up,' Milo ordered the battered dealer. 'You had better stay with him,' he said to Harwood.

'Don't worry, mate. I'll shoot the bastard if he makes any false moves.'

'Good man.'

Harwood's sympathy had reverted to 'I hate the scruffy unkempt little bastard' mode once again. It must be the pills wearing off, thought Harwood. He'd been on medication since his manic mood swings were becoming much more regular these days. The pair laughed as Harwood aimed his pistol at the scruffy dealer's chest.

A short while later, Harwood and Milo were ready to leave the premises. They warned the dealer to act normal as they walked down to the car, and not to try anything daft on the way. Having agreed to these terms, the scruffy dealer was placed in-between the two of them as they left the flat.

'I need to let them know that we're on our way,' said the dealer.

'No chance, not until we are a hell of a lot closer,' replied Milo.

They knew that ahead of them could well be a very long and difficult day. They began to make tracks out of the unkempt shit hole that they had just spent far too much time in. They moved along as swiftly as they could, trying to slip out unnoticed as they walked through the grotty, sticky corridors of the flats. Harwood tried not to breathe in too deeply as the smell of urine and a variety of other unpleasant odours assaulted his and Milo's nostrils. When they finally left the soiled, dank-smelling structure they all breathed deep sighs of relief.

'How can you put up with that stench?' said Milo.

The scruffy dealer just shrugged his shoulders as if to say, 'I don't have much of a choice, this is where I live.' That was just the way it was for the likes of him. Redfern was well-known for being a tough inner-city suburb.

Harwood took his time looking around to survey the area before walking to their means of transport. He made sure nobody was paying any attention to two white police officers manhandling a scruffy, part-aboriginal dealer towards the car. Milo had to admit that his BA series sedan version of the Falcon GT looked grand in its distinctive yet stylish yellow colour. With its 5.4 litre V8, 3 valves per cycle variable cam timing it was a real 'FPV', or Ford performance vehicle.

'Nice wheels, mate,' the scruffy dealer commented as Milo opened the back door.

'Yeah, I know, wipe your feet before you get in,' he

answered. Milo was extremely proud of his motor; an Australian classic, he called it. He loved cars and owned four of them, all Australian classics. Harwood could not give a shit about motor vehicles. He owned a beaten-up old Toyota Corolla that got him from A to B. In the great scheme of what they were up to, Harwood figured that the lower his profile was, the longer he would be able to get away with all the crap they seemed to be mixing in. Clearly, Milo liked to show off his success.

They drove away from 'The Block', as the locals called it, through the vicinity of Eveleigh Street, Caroline Street, Louis Street and Vine Street, driving slowly past Redfern Station, where a small gang of aboriginal youths were hanging around, watching as they drove on by.

'So where exactly in Mount Druitt do these muppets reside?' demanded Milo.

'I'll know it when we get nearer to the place,' said the dealer.

'I hope you do, because this is your last chance, boy. We know heaps of places to bury you out there if you're pissing us around.'

The scruffy dealer swallowed hard as he took in their latest warning. It would only take forty-five minutes to get out to Mount Druitt.

Harwood was sat in the back seat, keeping an eye on their rather anxious-looking, drug-dealing friend. He was thinking about how it was only a few short weeks ago that they'd had to lose another 'character' somewhere out in the bush. He watched Milo out of the corner of his eye and wondered how he kept so laid-back about it all. Harwood promised himself that this would be the last one – he would not be involved after this. He had to get clear of any more bloodshed and mayhem. He had put masses of money aside, but how could he tell his partner of seven years that he wanted out? It was impossible, he thought. He also realised that if this frightened dealer did not come up with the goods, Milo only had one way of sorting it out. Harwood hoped the dealer was not leading them up the garden path, because he could do with another nice few quid. Then he reckoned he might have almost enough cash to disappear for good. That's the first thing I will do, he thought. He was coming to comprehend that his moods, as unpredictable as they were, were nowhere near as manic as Milo's blackouts, which were now coming thick and fast. It was obvious that these habits were out of control, and surely they would not be able to keep up with the charade of it all at work. He knew that Sergeant McCabe was no fool. In all probability he was already onto them and their profitable sideline, and if he wasn't, he reckoned he soon would be. Anyway, that would be for another day – right now he had to focus on the task in hand.

14

What Have We Done?

England

Luke woke up later than usual the next morning. As he opened his eyes, it only took a few seconds for the awful memory of the previous night to return to the forefront of his mind. 'Got to get up and carry on as normal,' he said aloud. It had just gone 5 a.m. Going to work seemed a good idea – maybe none of last night's drama ever really happened. Who was Luke trying to kid – it had happened, all right. Nobody else in the house was up at this ungodly hour, which suited Luke down to the ground, as he did not feel like talking. However, he knew that soon he would have to act as if nothing had happened at all. In the bathroom he checked his reflection in the mirror. His eye, which had swollen up during the struggle, now looked fine thanks to the cold compress he'd applied when he'd got to Monks' place, everything else looked in order, even though he ached all over. After brushing his teeth, he felt ready to face the world.

To his surprise, when he shut the front door behind him Mr Kravis was waiting for him by his car. 'Are you okay, Luke?' he asked.

Though shocked to see his kindly neighbour out and about this early, Luke responded with a smile.

'Of course. A bit early to be out for a stroll, isn't it?'

Luke wondered if the old man knew anything. How could he? It had not even been reported yet, surely.

'I am just looking out for your welfare, son,' the old man said.

'Don't you worry, I'm fine.'

Old Mr Kravis smiled and then carried on his way.

Opening the shop that morning, Luke felt anxious about what the day held in store. He looked over his shoulder furtively as he picked up the newspapers; the headlines screamed out at him about the demise of a prominent local gangster. Entering the premises quickly, he went straight to the kitchen at the rear of the building, shaking almost uncontrollably. 'Take it easy,' he said aloud and then took a sharp intake of breath. It came as a shock to see what he had done written in print, but he knew that he had to chill out about it. 'Right, pull yourself together, Luke.' He repeated this three times, switched on the lights and opened for trading.

Later on at around ten, Shannon phoned to let Luke know that she had postponed her flight home for two weeks. He was pleased to hear from her, and they arranged to meet for dinner up west.

'Have you heard the latest?' Uncle Darren asked when he came into work.

'Sure have – it's all over the radio.'

'No one will miss that cunt.'

'No, I suppose not,' Luke said, then changed the subject.

Today was the day that Danny had been due to visit to tax him on his side venture. Darren knew this and decided not to mention it, as he suspected that Luke – or in his mind, more likely Monks – may be involved with last night's events. Luke seemed to be on edge all morning, Darren noticed, which only heightened his suspicions.

The work day rolled on by. Luke was generally quiet for most of it, and nobody from the Chilton mob came in to collect any monies from them. Darren was becoming more suspicious by the minute about his nephew. Monks turned up to see Luke, bowling in with a huge grin on his face. 'How are you, Darren – business good?' Uncle Darren did not think much of Monks, he knew he was bad news. But he was Luke's friend and so he always remained civil, though he kept their conversations to a bare minimum. 'It could always be busier,' he responded.

'Oh well, can I have a quick word, Luke?'

'Sure, come through the back.'

As he passed Darren, Monks gave him a patronising wink. Darren muttered something inaudible under his breath.

'You look ill, mate.'

'I feel it, mate,' admitted Luke.

'Listen, it's all sweet, nobody will ever suspect us,' Monks reassured him. He thought that Luke might be worried. Unlike Luke, he had enjoyed killing a top man – that was as good as it gets as far as he was concerned, especially as he felt they were untouchable. This can be a stepping-stone to greater things, thought Monks in his deluded mind.

'I cannot just forget, mate – we killed a man.'

Monks put his hand on Luke's shoulder.

'Just relax, it will all be history in a week,' he said.

'I hope you're right,' said Luke.

'Look, I've got a deal going down. I'll call you later.' Monks hugged Luke then smiled. 'We'll be top boys before you know it.'

Luke did not want to be a top boy; he only wanted to make a decent living and not have to deal with all this crap.

'See you, uncle,' said Monks as he left the shop, whistling. How – and more worryingly, why – is he so calm about it all while I am shitting a brick? thought Luke.

Darren was now certain that his nephew was involved somehow in what had transpired the day before, as he knew all about the mobile phone dealings and the late Danny Chilton's interest in them.

'You can talk to me, Luke,' he said, though he wasn't sure if he really wanted to know all the details.

'It's all right, it's all in hand,' Luke replied.

His uncle did not push it any further and told Luke to have the rest of the day off, as it seemed quiet. Luke thanked his uncle and offered to open in the morning.

'No, it's fine, just make sure you are here for midday.'

'Okay,' said Luke as he put on his coat. He rang Shannon and told her that he could meet her earlier than planned, about which she seemed pleased.

Driving through West London to get to his mum's on a Friday evening was a nightmare. Everybody was rushing home for the weekend. For the first time in the last twenty-four hours, Luke was not thinking about what he'd done to Danny Chilton. He was now completely infatuated with Shannon Rodman and couldn't wait to see her later. She would make him feel good and help him try to move on as quickly as possible. Eventually, having crawled through the gridlock, he arrived home. He felt different to the previous night when he got out of his car and walked to the house. Perhaps he was similar to Monks after all – could the guilt be easing this swiftly?

Old Mr Kravis was staring out of his front room window again. Luke acknowledged him with a wave, and he waved back. As he opened the door Luke thought about all the tales the old man used to tell him them when they were young – fascinating stories of how he and his young girlfriend, who became his wife, had to escape the Nazis during World War Two when they invaded Ukraine. They tried to seek out all the Jews and rounded up all his family and friends, most of whom ended up transported to the death camps, or into forced labour. Luke lapped it all up – the escape from the Nazis, the trek across Europe, ending up in England to live a good life – it all sounded exciting and filled with danger at every turn. Which of course it was,

116

though he often left out the horrific sights that he had witnessed. Oh, Mr Kravis loved telling all the kids about those dark times. He just wanted to teach them about the evil that men are capable of; he did not ever wish the slain to be forgotten. Besides, all young boys love to hear a good war story. Luke and Lindsay, Mr Kravis's only granddaughter, had heard them all.

Luke was in a reminiscent frame of mind at that moment as he went into the kitchen.

'Hello, mum,' he said, giving her a huge hug.

'What time did you get in last night?' she asked.

'Don't know, I can't remember – late.' Luke decided to go upstairs before he was given the third degree. He was thinking about one particular story of Mr Kravis's about how he escaped from the Ukraine – what a journey that must have been. He remembered how he'd had to kill three Nazis on the way, how he never saw his mother, father or younger sister ever again. How painful – knowing that while he had survived, his entire family, for all he knew, were dead. How on earth did a fourteen-year-old boy with his young girlfriend ever recover? They did, though. And then he wondered whatever had happened to Lindsay. She had gone to the Holy Land, that was all the old man would tell him. What did he mean by that? Was she fighting in Palestine or something, defending Jewish homelands? You never know, he thought, she had always held her grandfather in high regard and shared his love of the Jewish race. Perhaps I should speak to the old man and find out what Lindsay is up to these days, he pondered. Now would be a good chance to ask as the old man was just crossing the road to pop in for one of his chats with Julie Crooks.

Jack Chilton was at his mother's home, trying to console her in their hour of need. It was not how Jack had envisaged taking over the firm. He was always content to sit back, take his cut and contribute very little. Jack enjoyed taking part in most of the gratuitous and often unnecessary violence because he was a bully, but he never got involved in the running of the business. Danny looked out for him, so that was good enough. He certainly did not need any of the aggravation that had now landed in his lap.

'Who did this, son?' she sniffed.

'I don't know, mum.'

'Find them.'

'We will, they won't get far.'

At that she continued sobbing for her departed son. Jack had had enough. He was an emotionless soul at the best of times, but under no circumstances did he intend to let whoever killed Danny get away with it. He had sent the two men who were supposedly minding Danny around all the regular haunts searching for any information or hearsay. News, especially the death of a top villain, spread like wildfire and everybody now knew. Even though Jack was in deep shock and needed to grieve, he knew that he would have to strike quickly to catch and punish the perpetrators before any rival firms took the opportunity to step in and start to take over many, if not all, of the Chilton mob's business interests.

Rixon, on whom Danny used to rely the most, had made good progress on a couple of leads that he had followed up. Searching in-between the lowlifes and oily toe-rags of West London two names had popped up once or twice. He had remembered that Danny had made an appointment to speak with and arrange a pick-up of some money from one of these new kids on the block. He was pleased with the enquiries that he had made and decided to go for a pint and report to Jack Chilton first thing the next morning.

Mr Kravis settled down on the sofa in the Crooks' household, a warm mug of tea in his hands. Julie thought well of the old man, though she did feel that he seemed to be visiting a tad too often in the last week.

'Is everything all right?' she asked him.

'Yes, fine, I just worry about you all.'

'Now, don't be silly,' Julie said with a smile.

At this point Luke entered the front room, ready to go and meet Shannon.

'You'll be moving in soon,' he joked to the old man. Mr Kravis winked at him, and then he stood up to speak to Luke. Before he could say a thing Luke's mobile rang.

'Hello, mate.' Luke paused as he listened to the voice on the other end of the line. Then he went pale. 'Are you sure?' he said. The call ended and he turned off his phone and stood there, silent. Mr Kravis did not attempt to speak.

'What's wrong, love?' asked his mum.

'Nothing, I have to pop out. I'll see you later,' he said before hurrying out the door.

It did not take too long for Luke to get up west to meet with Shannon. They settled into a cosy pub off Old Compton Street. Luke tried not to think about what might happen if he stayed around, if the call he had taken had all the correct information.

'I'm coming to Australia with you,' were his first words to Shannon when he met her.

Shannon's eyes lit up. She had been going to ask him to come with her again that night. Now that he had suggested it, she was delighted.

'Cool, let's book flights.'

Luke had not even thought about living anywhere else other than London, but Australia sounded good right now.

'You love me, then?' she asked.

'Yes, I love you,' he said. And then they embraced. With their dark secrets locked away, both of them felt so safe in each other's arms.

*   *   *

Nothing of note happened for a couple of days, and so Luke and Monks thought the best thing to do would be to carry on as normal and remain in contact by phone. Monks was regularly checking in with Luke. He could not help but wonder if the whole situation was beginning to get to his pal. Luke had made enquires at Australia House about a visa. He was ready to go at any moment – he had plenty of cash stashed away and intended to get hold of quite a bit more. Shannon went to a bucket shop to get a pair of flights for a good price; everything was in place, they were just waiting on his holiday visa.

The media was intrigued by the slaughter of one of West London's gangsters. Fortunately for Luke and Monks the Metropolitan Police did not have the faintest idea that they were the hit men. All the usual routes were followed, but the only trail they found would turn out to be a false one. The police, in all their wisdom, were rounding up all the local villains, and to be fair the rogues they were bringing in to question genuinely were not trying to hide anything, as they did not have a clue who the killers could be, although they were all grateful to who did it. This was good news for Luke and Monks. On the flip side, though, one or two men did have a fair idea that they were involved. And one of them was biding his time before making himself known to them both.

Luke was in deep conversation with a sweet little old woman from White City estate who had come into the shop to buy her weekly pack of Berkeley Menthol. Luke often slipped an extra pack into her shopping bag as he knew her pension never went far. He was sure she knew he did this, but she never mentioned it. His uncle would go potty if he found out, but Luke always put a fiver in the till so he would never notice. He often helped the old boys and girls because he felt he should give a little back from time to time. His uncle was affluent enough to be able to swallow it. He waved at the old woman as she left the shop.

Luke's mobile started ringing. He answered the call and on the other end of the line was a nasal-sounding Australian, who explained to Luke that, due to his criminal record, at this time they would be unable to grant him a holiday visa. In that instant Luke's world came crashing down around him. He did not bother to listen to the rest of what the bureaucratic twat had left to say and simply ended the call. He began to panic as he realised his options were limited. He had to think fast – what could he do?

Meanwhile, Jack Chilton had been busy arranging his brother's funeral. He took some time out to speak with his brother's most trusted aide, Rixon.

'We won't touch then until after the funeral,' Jack instructed him in a low voice.

'I understand,' replied the driver solemnly.

Only Jack and Rixon the driver were aware of whom they suspected, and they wanted to keep everything low-key for the time being. Let them think they've got away with it – that was to be the arrangement.

15

Murder in Mount Druitt

Sydney

The sun was now at its peak. It was gone half past two and it was red hot. Luke was covered from head to toe in factor 25 sunscreen; no way was he going to burn. You only do that once, as most people learn. He was pouring suntan cream onto Shannon's shoulders and down onto her back when his Nokia mobile phone started to ring for the umpteenth time that day. Knowing it would be Monks, he wiped the slippery cream off his hands to answer the call.

'I've been trying to ring you all day. Where you been hiding, mate?'

'Nowhere, pal, just having a lazy day chilling on the beach with Shannon.'

'Have you seen the local rag?'

'No, why?'

'I suggest you take a peek at one. That chap we battered is in a bad way.'

Fucking liberty, Luke thought, I didn't batter the poor sod – he fucking did. Where the fuck did the 'we' come from?

'No worries, mate, I'm sure he'll be fine. After all, he's in the right place,' said Luke, trying to convince Monks that everything would be all right.

'Listen, mate, I'm going to have to pop over for a beer and a chat later this evening. Is that okay with you?' Monks asked Luke.

He could do without it, but Luke knew that if he said no he would still turn up anyway.

'Okay, what time? Not too early though, mate.'

'No, I'll meet you at about nine o' clock at your apartment.'

'All right, mate, I'll see you then, bye,' said Luke then, abruptly ending the call. Shannon turned to face Luke. 'What's he done now?'

'Nothing, as far as I know.' Luke did not like having to bullshit Shannon. She knew he was not going to tell her too much of what Monks had just spoken to him about, so she decided not to pry. 'Let's go and get something to eat,' she said, changing the subject. Great idea, Luke thought. A good meal would take his mind off the upcoming scenario for the rest of the afternoon.

Luke and Shannon got up and dusted off the sand. They were only a few metres away from the promenade so they decided to take a casual meander along The Corso, stopping to browse in a whole host of shops. They came across a decent-looking open plan bar where they stopped to have a spot of lunch. Luke had to decide on whether to come clean with Shannon about the incident that had taken place the previous week. They chose a table near the bar inside the spacious but oddly decorated dining area. The air-conditioning felt refreshing on their skin after three or maybe more hours in the sun. Their body temperatures began to cool down almost immediately. They'd had enough of sweltering all morning in the ferocious heat of a baking hot Australian sun. A short, fat cheerful waiter made his way over to them. Luke politely asked the man for a stubby of Victoria Bitter. Shannon ordered a glass of chardonnay. Luke took a long sip of the icy cold beer. Shannon did likewise. Luke placed his stubby bottle carefully back onto the exact spot where the residue had marked the table. He was certain that now would be a good time to reveal why he was late one night last week.

'I have something I need to tell you,' he began.

Shannon feared the worst. She was hoping that he wasn't about to inform her that he was seeing somebody else. She needn't have worried about that, as Luke adored her. He held his hand out to hers. Shannon kept her hands by her side.

Luke had always kept the reasons why he had to run away from England to himself. He would never want to hurt her with these facts. But he knew he had to let her know a little more detail about current events. He stared into her beautiful brown eyes and began to confess the gruesome particulars of what he and Monks had done.

'Shannon, you know that I love you more than life itself. Please hear me out. I have to let you know something terrible about what happened last week while I was out with Monks on the town.'

Those words sent a shiver down her spine. She knew that anything that involved that man could only mean bad news. She put her hand into his. She took a deep breath, primed her mind for the facts and then said, 'Tell me, Luke, what's wrong?'

Eventually Harwood and Milo reached their destination, directed by the nervous scruffy dealer. Harwood put his gun down the front of his denims as he got out of the car.

'Is this the place? You're not winding us up?' said Harwood apprehensively, taking a good look around the area. He didn't trust the scruffy dealer at all.

'Yeah, we're here. Can I call them now?'

Milo gestured to Harwood to come and speak to him. 'I don't know what to think mate,' he said, 'I reckon we've got to play it by ear.'

'Yeah, I'll trust the old gut instinct,' Harwood agreed as they got back in the car.

They did not intend to end up caught in a tricky situation. The air was extremely muggy today, a real intense heat. They observed the surroundings they found themselves in. It was quiet, a fair way from Mount Druitt Hospital and well away from the main thoroughfare. A dusty road off the beaten track led them towards the smart tidy building up in front of them. Driving halfway up the dusty track, Milo spotted the first of many CCTV cameras staring down on them. These blokes were clearly security conscious, he mused. Further down the track they pulled up and left the vehicle a good ten yards from the building. They began walking with assurance in the direction of the clubhouse.

'You are sure these blokes will have what we are searching for?' asked Harwood.

'Yeah, no worries boys, they have all the merchandise you are ever going to need, trust me.'

The problem with that is when somebody says 'Trust me', that statement does not always ring true. Harwood and Milo had been down that road more than once before.

A hulk of a man greeted them. Peter Maugham was his name. Milo kept just behind their scruffy associate. The first thing Harwood noticed as he scanned the man up and down was the fact that although this bloke had all the attributes of a mean-looking mother with a do-not-fuck-with-me demeanour, there were no patches on his waistcoat. This was unusual for a member of a motorcycle gang. He stood there at about 6 feet 6 inches high, with the largest beer belly you are ever likely to see. He had all the typical outlaw motorcycle gang look and feel about him, but no insignia to represent him or his gang. This could well be a problem if Harwood and Milo were to do business with these people, purely because they would not know who the fuck they were dealing with. Had the scruffy little bastard pulled one over on them? Well, we're here now, thought Harwood, I suppose we may as well go ahead and take the risk. They had guns with them if they needed to get out quick, but no doubt these bikers would have a fair old armoury too. This was a worry, an aspect they could not overlook. Who would they be crossing? Still, the scruffy dealer seemed at ease for the first time today, he observed. Was that a good or bad sign? Confusion reigned. Either way, they were about to find out.

'We aren't due a meet until next week,' said the biker. He did not look too happy to see the scruffy dealer.

He answered the biker, 'I know mate, but I've brought you some new shit-hot connections.' He was trying his best to look calm and convince Peter Maugham, the mean-looking beast of a man, with his bullshit.

'I don't know these two; they could be cops, for all I know,' Peter said.

'Do you think I would be stupid enough to bring cops out to see you, Pete? I haven't got a death wish, you know.' He laughed out loud, then turned to face Harwood and Milo, who were watching every move with the utmost caution.

'Hang on a minute.' The biker glanced at Harwood as he ducked inside. He completely ignored Milo, which really pissed him off. All three of them were left waiting outside the clubhouse. Nobody spoke. The scruffy dealer dared not look at either of his captors. Was he calling their bluff? Harwood and Milo anxiously wondered what would happen when the biker returned. Both of them were twitching to pull out their weapons. They did not have to wait long. Peter Maugham returned with another hard-looking biker named Michael 'Gibbo' Gibson. He was well over six foot – they all seemed tall – and had a long grey beard that stretched down to his chest. He also wore a regulation waistcoat, with no insignia. No club colours were visible, and of the two members of this group they had now seen there was still no sign of any identity. They knew all the outlaw motorcycle gangs by name, and of course their fearsome reputations. Harwood had slightly more experience in dealing with and recognising these types of people than Milo. He knew of all the bikies, ranging from the allegedly criminally active – such as Bandidos, Hells Angels, Comancheros, Gypsy Jokers, Nomads, Coffin Cheaters and even the new outlaw motorcycle gang named Notorious – to the plain old enthusiasts, like the Rebels, possibly the largest gang of bikers in the whole of Australia.

Anyway, the two bikers by now were standing outside, checking all three of them out. They took plenty of time to look them up and down, then turned to each other and discussed in a low, barely audible tone, so that neither Harwood, Milo nor the scruffy dealer could make out a word they were saying. Another look at them, one more whispered conversation.

'Okay, you trust these two, right? No messing about.'

'With my life Pete, I swear,' said the dealer. The man was not wrong; it could well be his life.

The security cameras were pointing directly at them, recording everything. Milo was very aware of this as they were invited into the inner sanctum. As they entered, Milo stepped to the rear, letting Harwood and the dealer lead the way after the bikers. They went through a double-steeled door, only to find themselves facing yet another armoured door and even more security cameras. Oddly, no other members of the gang were present at this time. Where could they all be? There had to be more than two of them. It just does not add up, thought Milo, who was watching and taking note of every inch of where they were going. Harwood was also entirely switched on and observing from the front end. He knew that when Milo took to the rear he would be on the ball behind them. The scruffy dealer was just winging it, hoping for the best. Peter Maugham stopped near the large double doors and turned to his sidekick Gibbo. Before leading them all into the clubhouse he stretched behind a counter and pulled out a sawn-off shotgun.

* * *

'When is that animal coming across to see you?' Shannon was visibly shaken by what Luke had just told her.

'I'm so sorry, I should have walked away. I promise that after tonight I'll tell him to stay away from us, I swear to you.'

Shannon paused for a moment, and then said, 'He has an aura of evil about him.'

'I know,' Luke answered.

'Promise me you mean what you have just said. I can't stand to be anywhere near him, Luke.'

'I'll keep him away from us. I have to see him later, though – you do appreciate that, don't you?'

Shannon looked up in the air, then back at him. 'I trust you, Luke; do what you have to do.'

He smiled with relief that she understood him. They got up to leave the restaurant, hand in hand. Shannon pulled Luke close to her and kissed him full on the mouth. Luke smiled as they tipped the waiter on their way out. Luke was trying not to worry about the meeting with his cohort later. He knew that he would not be able to tell him that their friendship was finished; Monks had far too much knowledge of his history.

At about nine-thirty, Luke was sitting in the apartment with Shannon. The intercom buzzed and he switched on the CCTV to see Monks waiting outside. He opened the security entrance for him. Monks smiled into the camera as he entered.

'Take him out for a while, and make sure that you get it through to him to disappear,' Shannon said.

'I'll talk to him. He'll get the message, babes, I promise you that much.'

He knew that this would be nigh-on impossible. Nevertheless, he had to try.

Monks waited as Luke went to open the door. Shannon

spoke to him as he passed her, 'Please, if he comes in here, don't let him stay here too long. I really can't stand him, Luke.'

'Okay, he won't be in here long.' He smiled at her then went to let him in. As Luke opened the door, he remembered yet again how close he had been to him since they were small, always looking out for each other. The trouble with all of it was, it had been for the most part one way. He often seemed to be getting Monks out of difficulty – only once or maybe twice had it ever been the other way round. There had always, at the back of Luke's mind, been the feeling that he owed Monks, even though he had never really known why.

'All right, Luke, have you thought about our little predicament?'

'No, Monks, I don't think I have really.'

'What's that supposed to mean, mate? We're in this together, you know.'

'That's the problem, Monks – you brought this grief onto me,' Luke said. Monks paused for a moment.

'Are you going to invite me in or what?'

Now it was Luke's turn to pause. Monks' tone changed in an instant.

'It has to be that bitch in there, I know she doesn't like me, she never fucking has, ever since we met her back home in England. The stuck up Australian cun –' Luke intervened. 'Monks, that's my girlfriend in there, don't talk about her in that way.' This was exactly the state of affairs Luke was hoping to avoid. He loved them both dearly, but he also knew that they hated each other with a passion. Why did this have to be so difficult? How could he choose between them?

Shannon could hear them and she was happy. She was glad Monks did not like her – she was hoping that it would make it easier for Luke, as she expected Luke to defend her honour and tell Monks to fuck off for good.

'Come on, Monks. Let's go down to the pub and talk this through sensibly. I can't afford to let Shannon know too much and I don't need to fall out with you, do I? Now think about it, pal, come on.'

Luke was trying desperately to diffuse any potential flashpoint between Monks and Shannon. He had to get Monks away from the apartment. Looking directly at Luke, Monks could see Shannon out of the corner of his eye, lurking in the hallway. He realised that he would never be able to convince Luke to stick with him while Shannon was nearby to counter his influence.

'You're right, mate. Let's go and sort it out over a couple of jars,' Monks said.

Luke glanced round and winked at Shannon then closed the door behind him. They went across to the elevator to make their way down to the wharf. Walking back into the living room, Shannon suddenly had an uneasy feeling. She could not quite figure out why.

Not too far away from the apartment was a cracking pub situated on Manly Wharf in which Luke and Monks had in the past shared a beer or two together. When they entered the popular waterfront location it seemed a little quiet for a warm Sunday night. Luke had been dreading this moment for a long time. He knew that sooner rather than later he would have to have this conversation with his dear but mentally unstable friend. Ordering two long cool lagers, he turned to Monks. 'You know what I'm going to say to you, don't you mate?' Even though Monks did know exactly what was coming, he still played ignorant with Luke.

'No mate, not a clue. No, if I'm honest, of course I do – you're worried about our little incident in The Hero of Waterloo, am I right?'

'Well, yeah, it's in the newspapers, mate. They reckon the bloke might die. It's not too good, is it?'

Luke thought that even a nutcase like Monks might feel

slightly concerned about the poor sod in a coma, not being able to move at all.

'As long as it doesn't come on top for us, I couldn't give a shit to be truthful with you, mate. The fat fucker was looking for trouble and he came unstuck.'

How do you answer that? thought Luke. But he was going to have to try. 'I think it would be a good idea if you cleared off for a while, just until the heat dies down.'

He could not think of a more polite way of gently telling Monks that it was time he fucked off and left him and Shannon alone. Watching his friend's mind absorbing this request had Luke feeling a little uneasy. He knew how Monks' mood could change all too quickly, although he was certain that Monks would never turn on him.

'It's that bird of yours, isn't it? Tell me the truth, Luke, I know she can't stand me.'

Luke was never going to let Monks know the fact that Shannon hated his guts. He knew it would not hurt him, but deep down he wasn't too sure how he would react if he found out that, ever since they met in bizarre circumstances in London six months ago, Shannon did not like, trust or want anything to do with the man at all. In addition, if Luke was honest, how could he not agree with her? The only reason that she even tolerated him was because of her relationship with Luke. Instead of telling Monks all this, he explained that no, it wasn't true and that she thought the world of him. Luke was a dreadful liar, but for once he managed to keep a rather convincing sympathetic look on his face.

Monks sighed and it seemed that he believed what Luke had just said to him. Then Luke witnessed something he had only seen in Monks once before, years ago: emotion. It was something Monks very rarely ever showed. He placed his head in his hands, then made a sobbing sound into his arms. It took him thirty seconds or so to compose himself. Luke was at a complete loss for what to say now.

'Come on, mate, you would miss me too much if I went away,' Monks said.

'Too true, I will, Monks, but we have to be sensible here, mate. More importantly, we do not want to be caught up in any more of this crazy shit, do we?'

Luke thought he was doing a fine job of making out that this would all be for the greater good. It even seemed for a moment that Monks was taking all of Luke's theories into consideration. Then, Monks paused to collect his thoughts. All of a sudden, as surely as night follows day, Monks changed his mind and decided that Luke had it all mixed up and that there was absolutely nothing to worry themselves about.

Harwood remained calm. He put his hand to his weapon. He had no fear – he loved the situation. If this monkey was going to play games, then Harwood was more than willing to accommodate the muppets. This was all part of the fun.

Pete pointed the sawn-off shotgun at the three of them and said, 'You can see what will happen if any of you are trying to take to the piss; I will waste the fucking three of you. So be warned, do not fuck about. Do you understand, you fucking mugs?' He laughed as he ushered them into the clubhouse, which looked tastelessly decorated. Harwood and Milo looked around for any signs of the club's identity. Neither of them came across any clues that would give them a hint of who these reprobates were. Could they be affiliated to any other outlaw motorcycle gang? They certainly hadn't heard of this biker gang with no name before. They all stood looking at each other silently in the bar area of the club-house. There were still only two members of the biker gang present which, taking into account that no one there knew each other, did appear to be slightly out of the ordinary.

Peter Maugham lowered his gun, leaving it just raised enough to let Harwood and Milo know that he could shoot them both quite easily from the angle he was facing them. The lure of some easy cash had tempted him to try to trust them. The scruffy dealer was beginning to unwind a little. Probably for the first time that day he actually felt at ease with the current situation. He thought that the power might have shifted in his direction. Maybe he could score a good deal for himself here – he sensed that he could play these four off against each other. After all, Harwood and Milo would not be able to let these bikers realise that they were cops, plus the bikers, in their pursuit of easy money in exchange for amphetamines, and various other cooked products, would not want to lose a new lucrative client. However, it then dawned on the stupid, scruffy dealer that none of them had any money on them; he had promised them that there would be lots of loot hidden away here. Shit, he thought – somebody is going to be pretty pissed off soon. His feeling of superiority passed quite suddenly as he now realised he was the only bloke present without a weapon of any sort.

'Right then, boys, to business,' Peter began. 'If you are tied up with this man, you are either mad, stupid or plain fucking desperate. Anyway, we don't really fucking care. As long as you have the money, that's good enough for us. So how much do you boys want to buy? Or more importantly, how much can you afford?'

Harwood had to think on his feet. The scruffy dealer had guaranteed them the ten grand that they were looking for. Now these dim-witted monkeys thought that they were there to buy drugs with the dishevelled little moron. Milo had to think fast as well. He was in harmony with Harwood – after all, they were one shit-hot team. For the past few years, they had almost perfected their system of extortion, blackmail and corruption. They reckoned they knew how to get the best deal out of what was now becoming an increasingly awkward predicament.

Harwood decided to speak up. 'You see, the problem we

have here is this: we turned up to see you blokes on the off chance, but I'm afraid we don't have any readies on us.'

The bikers looked at one another with disdain. Then Peter turned to Harwood and Milo and said, 'Then what the fuck are you dumb drongos doing here? Jay will always let me know in advance if he was on his way with a couple of mates to buy a load of gear. Out of the blue with no prior notice you come all the way up here with no fucking money – what type of fucking wankers are you?'

He then raised his shotgun to aim at Milo's head. Regrettably, this did not work out too well for Peter Maugham. This was to be the last deed of the mean-looking motherfucker's life. In the five seconds it took Peter Maugham to lift his arm, Harwood had pulled out his colt .380 from the front of his denims and shot the biker right between the eyes. Gibbo, in a blind state of panic, scrambled for his shooter. It was too late, though; enough time had elapsed for Milo to go for his weapon. Both of them now had their guns pointing at Gibbo, who stayed frozen to the spot. His hand reached for his gun, the scruffy dealer watched in abject fear, knowing he had no chance of gaining the upper hand in this dilemma as he still had no access to any type of weapon.

'Drop the fucking gun, now.' Gibbo did not hesitate; he dropped his gun straight away and instinctively raised his hands into the air.

'Where's the money kept?' Harwood demanded. 'No bullshit, pal, tell me now or you will soon be with your mate lying down there.'

Peter Maugham was stone cold dead, his brains splattered everywhere. The bullet had come out of the other side of his head – well, what remained of his skull – and was embedded in the wall directly behind him. By now an impatient and excitable Harwood was anxiously waiting on a response on where the money was located. Milo glared at Gibbo.

'Do you know where anything is? Where is the safe?' No answer was forthcoming from Gibbo. He just held his hands up in the air as still as you like; he had not moved an inch since he dropped his weapon. Then he chose to respond to Harwood's request.

'Are you fucking mad? The boys will be back here shortly, then you are dead. You don't know who you're messing with.'

That is damn right, thought Harwood; we do not have a clue which type of mental head cases we are robbing now. He had no time for this loony.

'Where's the fucking safe?' he barked. He then pulled the trigger and shot Gibbo in the right foot, blowing his big toe clean off.

'AAARGH … you bastard, my fuc –'

Harwood aimed the gun at Gibbo's other foot.

'Out through the back, through the back. AAARGH!' he screamed, clearly in absolute agony. The scruffy dealer raced through the double doors to retrieve the goods. As they waited for confirmation that Gibbo was telling the truth, Milo walked across to Gibbo, who was hopping around on his good foot. He picked up the discarded sawn-off shotgun and belted Gibbo square across the jaw, rendering him unconscious. He laughed as he watched his victim crash to the floor.

'That will shut him up for a bit,' he said. And then, with a casual swagger, he tossed the sawn-off shotgun over his right shoulder, feeling contented with his actions.

The scruffy dealer returned to the room in which they were standing with a grin from ear to ear.

'You will not believe this – the dopey bastards have only left the safe door open, and there is thousands in there, boys. We've hit the jackpot – at least a hundred grand, I reckon.'

The scruffy dealer had pulled it off. He believed that he had saved his skin.

'Go check it out. I'll stay put in case this lunatic wakes up too soon,' Harwood said, realising it could get tricky when the biker came to. He knew very well that he had to keep his eye on the ball.

'Right with you, I'll load up the cash,' agreed Milo. He went out with the scruffy dealer to bag up the takings. Gibbo began to stir. Harwood watched intently as he came slowly back to consciousness. Gibbo yelped aloud as the pain in his foot kicked in. Harwood trained his gun on him and walked over to the wounded biker, keeping him in his sight all the way. Then, calm as you please, he positioned himself directly above Gibbo. The realisation of what was about to happen to him hit Gibbo – he knew it was now pointless to cry out for any mercy. He could see it in Harwood's eyes. He composed himself for the end, and glared straight at Harwood with his last moments on this earth before him. He simply said to his executioner, 'The boys will find you.' He sneered as Harwood aimed the gun at him and mockingly said to the biker, 'Any last words?' Then, at point blank range, he pulled the trigger and for the second time that day blew a man's head off his shoulders.

'You boys don't even know my name. We're all partners now, right? We're all in this together. This is just the beginning, we're going to clean up boys, oh yes,' babbled the scruffy dealer. His sense of joy could not be underestimated, he was on cloud nine. They were driving away from the clubhouse, where two men lay dead. Harwood said to the scruffy dealer, 'Okay, what's your name? We only know you as a crack cocaine scumbag.'

'Yeah, but after what happened in there we are going to have to stick tight, you get me?'

'Fair dinkum, mate, so what's your name?' he repeated. Milo seemed curious, presuming he would have some complicated indigenous moniker. The scruffy dealer was excited at the prospect of joining this rogue police outfit. He told them, 'My name is Jay, it's Jay Edwards.' He seemed pleased at the thought of Harwood and Milo wanting to accept him as part of their exclusive unit.

'Well, Jay Edwards, it looks like you have pulled a rabbit out of a hat today, sunshine,' Milo said, then winked at Harwood as if he were mocking the scruffy dealer. He then continued, 'How many more contacts like that have you got, Mr Jay Edwards? More importantly, my friend, when are you going to be able to set up a meet with some of these losers?'

Jay then realised he might have cocked it all up again, as they were the only connections he had. Moreover, since they had just killed two members of this particular outlaw motorcycle gang he was hardly likely to venture out to this part of the state again anytime soon. He decided to be upfront with his brand new associates.

'To be honest, boys, that was where I used to get my entire stash. Now, after what has just happened, I would have thought it would not be possible for us to split up. I am with you boys one hundred percent. You can see I won't let you down.'

The car remained silent. Neither Harwood nor Milo responded. It seemed that the journey back to the city might continue in utter silence. Harwood knew that he and Milo needed to make a quick decision on what to do with their new accomplice, Mr Jay Edwards.

In the back of the Ford Falcon GT, Jay Edwards glanced anxiously at the two bent cops, who had taken the option of not communicating with him. He was concerned that he had made a big mistake by telling them that he had no more handy contacts. Now that they had killed in front of him, how would they perceive him? With a stroke of good fortune he may be safe just for the time being. He thought it might be in his best interest to remain silent in the back of the car until they hopefully dropped him off home in Redfern. He knew that if they did let him go for now he would have to disappear before they came back to him for another foray into the outlaw motorcycle world. Jay was starting to feel as if he had become useless to them, as he had while he was crying and begging on the floor of his tacky flat only a few hours earlier. Please take me home, he was now thinking. Jay Edwards's survival was his only pressing concern.

They were bearing towards Redfern, or so Jay Edwards thought for a while. He knew the route fairly well, as he had taken it a few times in the past. The silent treatment continued for an added five minutes. Jay was counting the seconds as they slowly ticked on by. Then Milo began to whisper to Harwood something that was almost inaudible as they changed direction. Jay swallowed hard – he could tell that something was afoot. He put his hand into his jacket pocket to feel for the CS gas canister he had picked up from the top of the safe they had robbed. These two didn't see him hide it as they were stashing all the money into the large rucksack he had also found in that room. Harwood turned to Jay and asked him a strange question, 'Do you want to go home today? If not, where would you like to be buried?'

The colour drained from his face in a split second as pure, abject fear consumed him. What can I do to escape their wrath? he thought. He moved swiftly and released the CS gas canister into the air. As he sprayed the toxic fumes Harwood felt the full effect. Milo swerved off the road and managed to stop the car crashing into the bollards on the side of the expressway. All three of them were struggling for fresh air, choking on the CS gas. Harwood had tears streaming from his eyes. Milo was coughing but still able to see fairly well. He turned to hit Jay Edwards, who had opened the car door and was half hanging out of the vehicle. A handful of motors passed them, blaring their horns at Milo, but none of them bothered to stop and offer any assistance to them. Jay was desperately rubbing the CS gas out of his eyes so that he could get away from their grasp. As Milo's vision cleared he saw his opportunity to nip the situation in the bud. He took his gun and shot Jay Edwards twice in the chest, killing him instantly.

Luckily for Harwood and Milo there were no more vehicles in the vicinity. Milo knew he had only a few seconds to move the body from the back seat into the boot of the car, but his partner was crying out in pain. He managed to grab a bottle of water and poured the liquid into Harwood's eyes.

'Quickly,' he said, 'we have to get him in the boot then get away now. Stay there while I move him.'

There were still no passing witnesses, so he jumped gazelle-like out of the driver's seat, round to the back of the car and opened the boot. He could now hear a vehicle approaching – they had very little time. Harwood scrambled out of the passenger's side. His eyes stung ferociously, but he had to help his partner. Frantically, he began kicking the body out of the back seat. A loud passing Toyota Corolla whizzed on by, without even giving them a second glance.

A deafening silence followed. They had a small window to shift the body. As they opened the back door the corpse slid out of the car, blood pumping sporadically out of the fatal wounds. Harwood and, to a lesser extent, Milo were still spluttering out the rancid gas from their throats. They just managed to move the dead weight round to the back of the car. Hearing another motor rumbling towards them, in one swinging movement they heaved the body into the boot and slammed it shut. Breathing heavily and soaked in their victim's blood, Harwood and Milo got back into the car without saying a word and shut the doors as an old BMW drove on by. They sat still until the coast was clear, then Milo, calm as a cucumber, started up the engine, flicked his indicator and pulled out to continue their journey Neither of them said a word. Even for these two, three murders in one day was completely off the scale. They now had to destroy a little more evidence – all in a day's work for them.

16

Can't Get a Visa

England

Luke was quite concerned about telling Shannon that he'd been refused entry to Australia. He thought it a liberty, frankly, considering it was not that long ago that all you needed was a criminal conviction to gain access to board a ship to the British ex-colony. He could not see a way around this dilemma. What could he do? Suddenly it came to him – Mr Kravis had contacts in immigration matters. He wondered if he could put him onto somebody. It had to be worth a shot, surely – there would be no harm in asking, would there? He needed to get this sorted out, so he made an excuse to his uncle and shot off home.

He rang the rickety old doorbell of Mr Kravis's well-maintained property. The old man shuffled along the hallway to answer the door.

'Hello, young man, how are you?'

'Good, can we talk?'

The old man could tell that Luke was upset, so he invited him in. Mr Kravis offered him a drink; Luke politely declined.

'I need a favour.'

Mr Kravis had known Luke was in some sort of trouble – the old man had seen it all before.

'I thought so. Come on in then, what is it?'

Luke swallowed hard then proceeded to explain. He told the old man everything that had happened; finishing with the difficulty he'd had obtaining a visa to enter Australia. Mr Kravis clapped his hands with excitement. 'I may be able to help you there,' he said. Luke's heart began to pump faster at the old man's reaction. God, it felt good to let someone else know. He felt like a huge weight had lifted from his shoulders. He knew that the old man would take his secret to the grave, such was the trust he had in him. Mr Kravis sighed then went over to the Welsh dresser in his living room. He fumbled around in a drawer for a while. 'Ah, here it is,' he exclaimed loudly. Returning to Luke, he began to explain what he must do.

It all seemed quite simple, Luke thought, as the old man went through with him which route he should take, and how to avoid looking conspicuous. Mr Kravis said that he would make all the arrangements for him to meet up with his granddaughter in Jerusalem. Luke was slightly bemused as to how the old man's granddaughter Lindsay, his childhood sweetheart, could possibly assist him in any way. More to the point, what was she doing in Jerusalem? He asked the old gent the question, the reply to which completely blew him away. He explained that all the tales and adventures that he told them all when they were small had always stuck with Lindsay while she was growing up. This was the reason why she disappeared all of a sudden when she turned eighteen, thought Luke – it was so she could serve the motherland, Israel. Even though he was thoroughly impressed by his friend's dedication in following her beliefs and acting upon them, he was still confused and did not understand how this would help his predicament. Then the old man let Luke into a secret that he swore him never to reveal. Lindsay had elevated her career to such a great height that she now worked for Israel exclusively. Intrigued by what he meant, Luke thought about it for a second or two, then concluded that she must be working for the Israeli secret service. Luke laughed as the old man repeated the information. He soon realised that he was serious.

'Unbelievable,' he exclaimed.

'Why would I make it up?'

Luke knew he was not pulling his leg.

'Give me a week,' Mr Kravis said. Luke nodded at the old man. He was stunned at the information that his friend would be able to lend a hand in this way. Mr Kravis went on to explain that the service he required would be expensive, and that Luke would have to be prepared to pay for the particular documentation. Not a problem, thought Luke, as he certainly had a fair amount of money put by.

'The Israeli secret service – really, I can't believe it.'

'Maybe, Luke, it could be true.'

He carried on explaining to Luke that, whoever she was working for, it was important to remain calm and not let the pressure catch him out. The golden rule was not to tell a soul about where he was going or why he was leaving. This would be the most difficult part, Mr Kravis went on to reiterate, as he couldn't reveal his whereabouts until, or in fact if, this business ever faded away. Luke agreed with him, realising the pain this would cause his family, but he knew that it would be better for all of them if he went away. Luke assumed that when it was safe he would be able to return to West London as if nothing had ever gone wrong at all. He had just decided to go travelling and see the world while he was able to, that was all.

While Luke was busy making plans to vanish from the parish, Monks was in the pub sinking a few lagers with the boys. He couldn't give a toss about the situation. Of course, he had no intention of letting anybody know that he was involved with the murder. Having said that, if in any way it would enhance his already impressive reputation in this part of London as an up-and-coming man to be feared, he certainly wouldn't be doing anything to stop them believing that he'd had a hand in Danny's demise. Marc Crompton would take that any day – it could only be good for future business, he surmised.

On a cold Thursday afternoon in October, the funeral procession had rolled on through West London. Luke was at work speaking to Shannon on his mobile about the up-coming trip to Australia. His uncle was attending the wake of Danny to show respect, he had told Luke – even though he couldn't stand the man when he was alive. Luke had been busy for the last couple of days preparing everything for the journey. He had withdrawn all his savings from his various accounts. Most importantly, he had arranged a day out in Bristol with Monks for one last mobile phone job before he packed it all in for good. Luke had promised himself that he would go straight once he landed down under. The old ways of ducking and diving did not appeal to him in a foreign country. He didn't want Shannon to think he was a dishonest sort of chap. He would keep all of his small-scale pieces of villainy away from her. He was in love with the girl and didn't wish to spoil the image that he had created.

'Hello, mate, all set for tomorrow?' Monks shouted loudly as he bowled into the shop, full of beans as usual.

Luke quickly ended his call and answered his pal. 'I can't wait to get down there.'

'All right, do you fancy a pint later?' He did not, but he didn't want Monks to think anything was up.

'Yeah, I'll be there around seven.'

'Okay, catch you then.' Monks turned on his heel and was on his way. Luke took his phone back out and redialled Shannon to finish making their arrangements, which were now far more pressing.

Jack Chilton left his grieving mother in his aunt's capable

hands as he left the wake briefly. He had some urgent business to attend to concerning his late brother. Rixon, who had now become Jack's right-hand man, informed him that he'd established a contact who may be able to confirm his hunch as to who killed Danny.

Another weekend had passed by and all of Luke's travel arrangements were now in place. He had worked it out so that Shannon would arrive in Sydney by a week on Friday, giving her lots of time to organise somewhere for them to live. Luke would be taking a longer route to avoid detection. He had to visit Israel to pick up certain documents, which would be false but should allow him to gain entry to Australia. Shannon was more than happy to go along with all this, as she needed to leave London as soon as possible. The worry of her little mishap in Soho was getting to her and she yearned to be home, away from any possibility of the law tracking her down as some sort of sex case lunatic. Neither of them had yet revealed to the other the reasons why they both had to skip London.

Monks and Luke were sitting in the living room of Monks' house sharing out the spoils of a rather successful raid over in the West Country. They had amassed so many phones in a short space of time in Bristol that they left there early, crossed the border into Wales and cleaned up in Cardiff as well. They laughed hard with one another as Luke calculated that they had cleared over three thousand pounds each. Considering this was to be his last escapade on the wrong side of the law, Luke started to think that he would miss the edgy, dangerous activities that he got up to with his pal. But this was to be the end of an era, he thought – time to move on. He couldn't wait. He was due to begin his journey in two days' time. He would see Shannon off in the morning, tie up a few loose ends, go through all the details with Mr Kravis and then be on his way to paradise, or so he presumed.

Monks had not sussed that his mate was about to break up the partnership, but he couldn't help but notice that Luke did seem to be hiding something from him. He asked Luke if everything was okay, to which Luke laughed and told him life couldn't be better. Monks resigned himself to the fact that he must be imagining it. Of course they were all right – soon they would be the talk of the underworld, or so he thought.

17

Locked-in Syndrome

Sydney

Nearly three weeks had now passed since Paul Symonds was hospitalised. Kerry Symonds had spent most of that time praying around the clock for her comatose brother. All the staff who worked in the intensive care unit at St Vincent's Hospital, Victoria Street, Darlinghurst, had comforted her. Dr Robb had the grim task of informing Kerry of the latest reports. He prepared the documentation on his patient and entered the room.

'Good morning, Miss Symonds. I have here the test results on your brother. Please take a seat.'

Kerry sat on the corner chair nearest to her sick brother while Dr Robb explained the current state of affairs to her.

'The results of our tests our now conclusive, Miss Symonds. I have to inform you that Mr Symonds is in a state which is known as locked-in syndrome.'

Kerry, still not any the wiser, just asked politely for some detail.

'Well, basically,' Dr Robb tried to explain, 'the patient, your brother, can think, hear and feel. But regrettably his brain damage leaves him unable to speak or move any of his limbs.'

'So where does that leave him – in a care situation?'

Dr Robb went on to specify further. 'Often, the only part of the body sufferers of the syndrome are able to move are the eyes. This is only possible because the nerves that connect the brain to the eyes are intact. This condition is extremely rare. You see, the lower brain and brain stem are damaged; nevertheless, the upper brain, with its higher mental functions, is left intact, allowing eye movement. It's possible that he may even be able to blink.'

Kerry was stunned. 'What does this mean, what can I do?'

Dr Robb went on further. 'I am afraid that the survival rate for this condition is very low.'

Kerry interrupted the doctor. 'Please, doctor, may I have some time alone with my brother?'

'Of course, I will give you a little space with your thoughts,' he said, then left the room.

Kerry had heard of locked-in syndrome. She remembered reading an article about it once. Her brother would be living in what an expert described as the closest thing a person could experience to being buried alive. She began to weep, as she realised how frightened her brother must be. She called Dr Robb back in.

'Do you think he will know we are talking about him?' she asked, to which he replied with a resounding, 'Yes – all our research says that he can.'

Kerry turned to her brother, 'I am going to get a cup of tea, Paul, I won't be long.' She gestured to the doctor to follow her. He duly obliged. Once they were both outside the intensive care unit Kerry began to speak to Dr Robb.

'You said, before, that it would be kinder for my brother to switch off the ventilator than it is keeping him alive.'

'Yes, I still believe that is correct – in a professional view, of course.'

'Very well. How much longer will he be able to live in the condition he is in at the moment?'

She was looking at Dr Robb. In her heart, Kerry felt that

the intelligence he was about to share would not be what she wanted to hear.

'The best case scenario, I would expect, for Paul, would be an absolute maximum length of support-assisted life of, I am sorry to say, no more than four months.'

He paused for a second then continued, 'Sadly, nine out of ten patients with this syndrome would not have been able to hold on as long as Paul has.'

Kerry thanked Dr Robb for his diagnosis, then requested to go and talk to her brother to try to make a decision. Dr Robb understood completely. She walked back to the intensive care unit alone.

Kerry was down on her knees, begging for forgiveness from the Lord. Standing up, she wiped the tears away from her eyes. She began stroking her poorly brother's forehead as if to soothe him. Kerry had made her decision. 'Paul, the doctors all say you can hear me. You know, you are going to get much better, but it is going to take a while to make a full recovery.' Kerry had never not told the truth before, but she thought that telling him this would help make his passing easier, that he would not know that she had given them permission to turn off the life support machine.

Many more tears were waiting to flow, but she was determined to stay strong until the end. 'Now, we are just going to adjust these pillows for you.' Then she gave the agreed signal to the doctor to switch off the ventilator. Kerry leaned over to comfort Paul Symonds in what would be his final moments.

Five minutes later, Dr Robb stood next to her and softly told her that her beloved brother had gone. She kissed her brother, then swore to him, 'Whoever did this to you will not get away with it. I promise I will find them. They will pay, as God is my witness, they will pay.'

She then broke down and sobbed uncontrollably, with the pain of her loss and her anger. If only her parents could be there just for a day with her, to try to help her absorb some of the unbearable pain. Paul Carl Symonds died at 5.42 on a Sunday evening. He was twenty-nine years old.

18

Time to Leave

England

Shannon had all her bags packed and was ready for the off. She had enjoyed her time in England, but she would be glad to get home. Although she had no family she was aware of, she was looking forward to seeing Debbie, the friend she grew up with in the children's home in Sydney. They had remained in contact regularly over the years, a bond that had lasted following some of the nightmarish memories they shared. Shannon told Debbie that after a short stopover in Hong Kong she would be arriving in Sydney around midday. Debbie, talking excitedly on the other end of the phone, promised to meet her at the airport, as she couldn't wait to see her and hear all about her travels overseas. This gave Shannon a warm feeling inside – she was also looking forward to catching up with her childhood friend, and she so wanted Luke to meet her and settle down by the ocean.

Luke's emotions were on top of him as he waved Shannon off at Heathrow Airport. She hugged him and promised him that by the time he arrived, she would have a place by the ocean ready and waiting for him. Luke felt butterflies in his stomach, as he could not be certain that he would even get to Australia with all the problems currently happening in West London. But now was not the time to worry about that – he was just pleased that he had Shannon out of the away before any issues caught up with him.

As soon as she passed through into Departures, Luke raced out of the airport to get back to his uncle's shop. It was to be his last day working for him. He couldn't let anyone know that he was leaving; he had to act as if everything was okay. Only Mr Kravis had any idea of what he was about to do, and he would have to see him at some point later that day. Mr Kravis was busy at home making all of the final arrangements for Luke's escape. He was chatting away to his grand-daughter, who was pleased to be of assistance to her first boyfriend. They were organising where he would have to meet up with her in Jerusalem and collect the goods for the tricky part of the journey.

Jack Chilton had been busy plotting against Rixon and Pug, both of whom he particularly blamed for not minding his brother while walking his dogs. What they did not know was that he had planned it so that one of them would be found responsible for the attacks and the disposal of the evidence. Jack had arranged it so that the police would be able to catch up with Pug, the co-driver, and charge him for the said offences. This was completely against everything his brother had stood for, but Jack had always had dealings with the Old Bill. Nobody would ever have suspected this, but Jack always felt that it never did any harm to keep in with a few bent coppers – I scratch your back, you scratch mine, that sort of thing. Moreover, he thought it would be a simple way of punishing the Pug for his own fatal mistake. He had separate plans for Rixon. He would deal with him at another time, as for now he was still of use. As he finalised all the details for the next morning, Jack felt eager to get revenge for Danny's demise.

Back at the shop, Luke was serving one of his favourite older customers from off the estate, a sprightly old girl who no doubt back in her day liked a gin and a giggle. Luke would miss all the banter and friendships he had built up over the years, working for his uncle. It just did not feel like a job. He had such camaraderie with most of the customers. Oh well, he thought, never look back. The future was bright; he did not want to start moping about and getting sentimental. Turning away from the till he faced his uncle.

'Will it be okay if I pick up my week's money tonight?' he requested.

'No problem,' replied Darren. Luke turned back to the till, opened it and counted out his week's money.

Later that evening, after Luke had closed the shop for the last time, he stopped in to see Mr Kravis before he went home. The old man had been expecting him. They went into the living room and he went through the timetable and procedure with Luke, making sure that he understood every detail. Finally, everything was in place. He stood up and thanked Mr Kravis for all he had done to help him. The old man rose to his feet and hugged Luke as if he were his own flesh and blood. As the two of them embraced, Mr Kravis promised Luke that he would take good care of his mother and Mickey for him, and that he would not tell a soul where he had gone unless Luke informed him that it was okay to do so. Luke knew that he was dealing with a good man, and that he would keep his word. He said goodbye and left to cross the road to take his family out for what felt like the Last Supper.

Julie and Mickey were all set to go out as Luke came in.

'Let me take a shower, and then we're off,' he said as he ran up the stairs.

'Okay love, no rush.' Julie was touching up her nails. It did not take Luke long to get ready, as he wanted to spend as much time as he could with them tonight. He decided to take them up to Covent Garden; Mickey loved it up there. He liked to walk among the tourists and mingle with the crowds.

He enjoyed watching all the people hanging around, waiting to enter the theatres, sharing a drink in the many pubs and bars. Luke had picked a restaurant that his mother had always wanted to visit. He had even hired a town car to drive them around, much to his brother's liking. This was to be a special evening, as Luke was not sure when he would be seeing them again.

They arrived in Covent Garden half an hour after they left the house. Julie was inquisitive as to why they were getting all this special treatment – it wasn't anyone's birthday or a special occasion that she had forgotten, was it? As they all got out of the car she asked her son what it was all for, to which Luke simply replied, 'Because I want to show you both how much I love you.' Julie was almost moved to tears at her lovely boy's wonderful sentiment. Mickey hugged his mum and Luke as they stood outside the restaurant together. Holding on tight, Luke kept his emotions in check. They entered the classy restaurant, all three of them looking forward to a fine dinner and most of all a great night in the West End in what they all thought was the finest and most vibrant city in the world. For Luke, it might well be the last occasion he would be able to spend any quality time with them.

The next morning, Luke awoke an hour earlier than he would normally rise if he were opening the shop. He wanted to get up early so he could take a good look around Shepherd's Bush before he left. He made a cup of tea, and then checked he had packed all the necessary clothes and had all of his cash tucked away in one of his holdalls. As he finished drinking his tea, the time had come to leave his home. He went outside and loaded up his car with his luggage. He had decided that he would drive to King's Cross. The tax on his car was due to run out at the end of the month and its second year service was due, so he reckoned he would dump it in the car park as he would not be using it again.

Now came the hardest part. He went back upstairs into his

mother's bedroom. Luke entered the bedroom ever so quietly, so as not to wake her. Moving slowly across to her, he leaned down and gently kissed her on the forehead. Taking a minute, he stopped so he could admire her – such a strong, independent woman, who had sacrificed a great deal to look after him and his brother. Beyond any doubt he was in awe of this incredible woman who was his mother. He kissed her once more then he silently left her sleeping. On the way to the top of the stairs he went into Mickey's room. He lay fast asleep on top of the duvet in his Queens Park Rangers home kit. This brought a lump to Luke's throat, knowing that he would not be taking him to the football any more. They were playing away at Reading on Saturday, and Luke had promised to take Mickey down the M4 to watch that game. The battle of the hoops, Mickey had called it, because both teams wore identical blue and white hooped shirts. Still, this wasn't to be. Luke kissed his little brother goodbye and, with tears welling up in his eyes, turned and walked out of his room.

As Luke closed the front door behind him and walked to his car he glanced across the road. Mr Kravis was staring out of his window at him. They both waved at the same time. Luke wiped the tears from his eyes, got in his car and took one last look at where he had grown up and shared such happy and sad times. He started up the engine and without looking back began driving away from the estate. He turned the corner at the end of the road into Shepherd's Bush Green, and headed across London for the start of a voyage into who knew what.

At around the same time, Jack Chilton stepped into the back of his Bentley He sat down then said to Rixon, 'We'll go and do Crooks first.'

19

Pain of a Victim

Sydney

The post-mortem confirmed everything. Locked-in syndrome was the official line that the hospital had instructed Dr Robb to tell Kerry. Although this was not the actual cause of death, it had helped her make the difficult decision to switch off the ventilator that was keeping him alive.

Ten painful days had passed and Kerry Symonds was now preparing for the funeral of her brother. Kerry had not spoken to Melissa, her oldest and most trusted friend, for a little while. With no family to turn to, Kerry had got in touch with her for some much-needed support. The hearse waited patiently outside the house as the mourners walked on past Paul Symonds' coffin. It was all performed in the strict Catholic tradition. Kerry had been praying all morning for her departing brother's soul. She realised that it was one of life's cruel acts that not everyone lives a long, fulfilling life. She had promised herself that she would not shed any tears until they had laid Paul to rest.

It was now time for the coffin to make its way out to the hearse. Four big strong pall-bearers were required, all of whom were close to Paul, to lift and carry the coffin. Two of them had been there on the fateful night that Paul had gone into The Hero of Waterloo to sort Monks out – the young loudmouth and Dave, who was Paul's best mate. Both of them were racked with guilt because they had not come to his aid on that critical evening. Lifting the heavy man up was not easy but they managed to carry him on through to his final journey. Kerry looked as dignified as anyone can in such circumstances. Melissa held onto her hand and squeezed it tightly. That gave Kerry enormous strength as she led the mourners out to the waiting cars. The funeral director had been so kind in arranging the finest details for her. He accompanied her to the leading hearse and explained to her that it would only be a short trip. She had been dreading this part of her brother's journey to his final resting place. Still, she held her head high as the funeral director opened the car door for her. As she sat inside Melissa kept hold of her hand as they waited for the other mourners to enter their vehicles.

Kerry remembered her promise to even the score for Paul's murder. She was filling up with hatred for whoever did this to him. Wiping a tear away she calmed down and tried to lose the abhorrence that was building up inside her. She had to remain calm for the service. Dignity was very important to her. She would be arriving at the head of the funeral convoy in no time at all and her head was swimming with unchristian thoughts, which was most unlike her. Kerry waited for her door to open. She crossed herself and asked the good Lord to give her strength. Melissa followed as Kerry stepped out of the leading car, keeping her composure. She was stunned to see how many people were already there. A crowd of around one hundred had turned out to pay their final respects to her brother. But even so, in her darkest hour she would have felt so alone if it wasn't for Melissa, who was a tower of strength as she kissed her and told her, 'Stay strong; remember what we've overcome before.' She stood up tall and thanked her for being there in her hour of need. Looking at all the mourners who had gathered, it was clear to Kerry that even though Paul Carl Symonds had been a bit of a rascal in his relatively short lifetime, he was evidently quite a well-thought of man.

With her friend holding her upright she made her way slowly into the chapel. The emotion of the sad occasion now started to move her friend as well. The chapel filled up quickly behind her; it had got to the point where it was bursting at the seams, with only standing room left. The priest suggested that the doors remained open so that the many mourners would be able to hear the service from outside the chapel. The service seemed to pass by quickly and was over in around about an hour. Throughout, Kerry hung onto her dear friend, just managing to maintain her dignity and poise.

After the service the oak-panelled coffin was rolled away to the crematorium, a song by INXS playing to accompany her brother as he disappeared into the distance. Kerry had held her emotions intact with the help of her friend up until this very point, but now she breathed in deeply, and as she breathed out the tears inevitably started to flow. She wailed aloud for her much-loved brother. Her friend placed an arm around her shoulder to try to offer a small amount of comfort at this overwhelming moment in time. The congregation began to stand, waiting for the signal to leave as Father Michael led Kerry through to the chapel of rest.

The mourners all remained outside, waiting patiently to offer their condolences to Kerry, who was still inside praying a touch more with Father Michael. She gathered her thoughts, then waited a moment before preparing to go outside the chapel to thank the large turnout for giving up their free time to attend this sombre occasion. Father Michael asked if she was ready as he took her arm and walked out with her and Melissa. He hoped he would be able to give her a little comfort and help to steer her throughout this sombre task. Feeling somewhat more composed, Kerry was now ready to acknowledge and invite all the mourners back to her home for Paul Carl Symonds' wake.

At the wake a large contingent were milling about, drinking and eating the excellent finger buffet Kerry had prepared the night before. Almost all the food was disappearing as quickly as she could replace the empty plates in her front room. She did not mind, though, she was just pleased that so many people had come to her humble home to pay their respects.

Although she was older than her brother, Kerry Symonds was a good-looking girl. She wore very little make-up, but most people would say that she had a certain attractive look about her. This had not gone unnoticed by Harwood, who felt that he should attend the wake as he and Milo had been called to the scene on the night of the attack. Harwood liked Kerry. He was impressed by how she had handled the tragic situation. He sipped his drink then made his way over to Kerry to offer his sympathy.

'Where are you going, mate?' Milo piped up.

'I'm just going to speak to Kerry, to let her know the latest information.'

'Are you sure this is the right time, mate?' said Milo, stuffing another handful of cocktail sausages into his mouth. He shook his head disapprovingly as Harwood walked across the floor. Harwood approached Kerry as she was thanking a couple more mourners for paying their respects. He stood just to the right of Kerry, waiting patiently for his opportunity to speak. Kerry noticed him standing there; she could see he looked slightly nervous, which she found quite sweet. On a day like this, watching this shy police officer acting so nervously cheered Kerry up a touch. She had found Harwood to be quite helpful in dealing with her brother's sad demise. In fact, although she had always had a deep religious calling, she had found herself becoming quite fond of the caring – or so he portrayed himself – police officer.

'Hello, Police Constable Harwood, so kind of you to come.'

'Absolutely, Miss Symonds, I felt that I should as we are on the case.'

Melissa sensed that these two might want to speak to each other alone, so she moved quietly away to make small talk with some other mourners. A slightly awkward pause ensued before Harwood spoke again.

'I realise that this is not the time to discuss the proceedings –'

'Well, let's not discuss it, then,' she interrupted him. Harwood went red and apologised to her. She actually felt a sense of relief at what she saw as a humorous comment, but she could see he looked embarrassed.

'No, Mr Harwood, please – you may let me know what is on your mind.' Again, she felt a sense of well-being at having relieved the pressure of the awkward situation. He cleared his throat and told her the news.

'The latest information is that we have managed to track an image of the man who killed your brother.'

Her mood changed. For a second or two she had felt safe in Harwood's presence and had forgotten her grief, but in that instant it returned. She stopped him again; she did not want to speak about such things at this time, because she found herself quite attracted to Harwood. At this point Milo came across to join them. She politely thanked him for his assistance in the investigation, although she found that she could not warm to this police officer as she had Harwood. Politely, Harwood made his excuses and said goodbye. He promised to speak to her as soon as they knew more details. Kerry smiled and thanked them once more. She hoped that she would be seeing Harwood again shortly. Then she began looking around for her friend. As they left the wake Milo taunted Harwood. He had noticed that his partner had obviously fallen for the deceased's sister. Harwood just grinned at his colleague.

159

'Come on, you muppet, we still have to tidy up that last piece of evidence left over from Redfern,' he said.

'No worries, mate. Let's get it done.' They walked back out to the parked police squad car.

20

Where's Luke Gone?

England

Jack Chilton was fuming. He had waited a substantial time to avenge his brother; well, three weeks, to be exact. Now that he had come to resolve the matter, he couldn't find the culprit. Uncle Darren explained to him that it was Luke's day off. Jack had to accept that as fair enough, so he told Darren that there was nothing to worry about and he would catch up with Luke later. Darren was wise enough to know that Jack Chilton didn't usually turn up without good reason, so as soon as he left he tried to warn Luke that something was wrong. But by the time this happened, Luke had ditched his phone in pieces at King's Cross Station. When he couldn't get through, Darren was left in limbo as to what he should do.

Meanwhile, Jack went to wait and watch at Luke's home for over two and a half hours. Rixon pointed out to Jack that opposite to where they were waiting for Luke to appear an old man was constantly looking out of his window, keeping an eye on them. Jack scratched his chin and thought that they may have to change tactics with the nosy old sod staring at them. With no sign of Luke coming out of the house in the near future he thought it best to move on. The fact that the meddling old man had kept on looking at them had riled him big style, but he had to make it look as if nothing was wrong. He glanced up at the old man and waved at him. Mr Kravis hid behind the curtain. Then Jack made the decision that they would leave Luke until tomorrow. 'Let's go see Monks,' he growled, pissed off that Luke was not around. Jack couldn't have guessed that at that time Luke was sat aboard the Eurostar to Paris. He had booked a first-class ticket, thinking he would start his journey in style, and smoothly sipped Earl Grey tea as the train raced under the English Channel, heading for France.

Monks rose out of some one night stand's bed at 10 a.m. He saw that she had left a small note with love hearts and soppy crap written all over it. He didn't even bother to read it, he just got dressed and went home. He had no intention of seeing her again; she was only another notch on his bedpost. That was why he always went back to the girl's place on these occasions, so that there was no chance of any of them ever knowing where he lived. He never intended to fuck them again after the first one. It was just his way – fuck them and leave them. No soppy tart was going to tie Monks down, as he often boasted to his mates. Mind you, last night's bunk-up was a good one. She certainly was game, thought Monks as he wandered off into Woolwich, looking to get back to West London.

Jumping off the Tube, Monks strolled through the station feeling pleased with last night's conquest. As he got near to his home, he began to feel slightly uneasy. He sensed danger; he was sure that someone was following him. When he arrived at his house, he cautiously entered the building. Keeping his wits about him, he made his way little by little into his home. Everything on the surface seemed normal, but he still didn't feel safe. He went to the back of his front room and picked up his sturdy cosh just in case somebody was lurking somewhere inside, waiting to pounce. Why did he feel so ill at ease? He began to relax as nothing had moved and there was no sign of any intruders. Looking out of his window, though, he saw Jack Chilton's Bentley pull up. This confirmed his uneasy sensation. He knew why they were there; they must know. Now it was time either to admit the truth or deny all knowledge. One thing he decided was that he would face them at some point and he would do that without any fear. The doorbell rang. Monks did not hesitate; he went to answer it straight away as he had made up his mind what he was going to do. This could be his moment of destiny.

The train pulled into Paris Gare du Nord. Luke made it across town to Gare de l'Est with forty-five minutes to spare before his connection, which would take him to Frankfurt and then on to Vienna. He looked around the old station for a bar as he fancied a beer to help kill a bit of time, just a small one to take off the edge. He wondered if anyone in London had realised he had left yet. He felt guilty about not telling his family why he was certain that he had to leave. Would Monks have sussed anything out and visited all their regular haunts to talk about making some money? Probably not, he thought, he only left London a couple of hours ago. Why am I thinking like this? he asked himself, and then stepped inside a cafe for that beer.

Mr Kravis sat drinking his tea before popping over the road to check on Julie and Mickey. He realised that Jack and his associates would be coming around sooner rather than later to look for Luke, so on reflection he wanted to try to help deflect any problems that may occur, to the best of his ability. He realised that he was no physical match for the men when they came calling, but he certainly knew a thing or two about diverting the blame elsewhere. This was something he had learned when he had to deceive and then flee from the Nazis back in the Ukraine.

*   *   *

Luke checked the time and then went across to the ticket office. When he got to the ticket booth, he managed to converse with the rather stern-looking woman behind the thick plate glass using the basic French he had picked up in school: a polite 'Bonjour' and 'May I buy a fare for a train to Vienna?'. This was where he had planned for the trail to go cold if the police, or more worryingly Jack and his crew, had decided to hunt him down. Paris was as far as they could pursue him. The stern woman hardly gave him a second glance as she took his money and handed him his ticket.

'*Merci,*' he said in a convincing French accent as he turned to leave. Luke checked he had the right platform then proceeded to board the smart French train. He sauntered down the carriage and found an empty seat by the window. He settled down and closed his eyes to catch some sleep. Luke woke from his slumber some time later; he had managed to sleep through most of France as the train was approaching the German border. Rubbing his eyes, he pulled out his map to see if he could work out how long it would take until they would be pulling into Frankfurt in Germany. It was not too far away. Amazing, he thought – a while ago he was sitting at King's Cross and now he was halfway through Europe. He decided that he would catch another forty winks, and settled back into his comfortable seat for a while longer.

The train came to a halt. Luke remained in his seat as most of the passengers in the carriage he sat in started to vacate. A message was bellowing out over the muffled intercom, but Luke did not understand what the man was saying. Not that it mattered, as he clearly had some distance to go until he had to change trains. He listened carefully anyway, as he was bored of sitting on the train with nothing to do but sleep, wake up briefly and watch unknown towns whizzing past him.

Two minutes passed and they were off again. Luke began checking his itinerary for the umpteenth time. A well-dressed German man spoke to him and then sat down next to him. Luke smiled politely then pretended to go to sleep, so that he could avoid getting into a pointless conversation with the man.

Monks' meeting with Jack and the boys all went very well. He surprised himself with the laid-back way that he had dealt with the matter. Jack seemed to believe him that it was always Luke's intention to kill Danny from the start. Monks had persuaded Jack that Luke had come to him boasting that he had done in the top man, and that it would only be a matter of time until he would catch up with Jack too. Nevertheless, he still had to be careful, as it could all still catch up with him if he could not manage to remember his story. Mugs, they must be fucking mugs, Monks thought. I should have done this right from the start, he was thinking – I've cracked it. This was exactly what he wanted. He knew that Luke would probably go underground. It was after their last trip down to the West Country, he could see it in his eyes that he was planning to get on his toes. He could be taking a huge risk presuming that he had already left, but if Monks knew anybody inside out it was his closest friend. The friend who he had now quite happily betrayed to save his own skin, giving him the chance to rise quickly through the ranks of the most feared firm in West London. Or so he would hope. The rumour had gone around that a lone hit man had killed Danny, so Monks felt sure now that nobody would suspect him.

Arriving in Vienna, Luke got up and started to remove his luggage from the racks above him. There was only one other passenger left in his carriage. He had to rush to meet the connection or he would not be able to get to Istanbul as quickly as he would have hoped. He need not have worried, as the service that he required for the journey to Istanbul had been delayed for twenty minutes, giving Luke some extra time to get his luggage sorted out. He found another window seat and settled down for the 653-mile trip to Belgrade, carrying on through Serbia, passing Sofia in Bulgaria and then finally down into Istanbul, where he had details of a small hotel lined up for two nights. He was hoping for a touch of breathing space from all this hopping from train to train which, in-between all the sleep he had caught up on, had become quite tiresome.

When Monks knocked on the door of the Crooks' house Julie came to answer. She seemed pleased to see him. 'Oh, where is he?' she immediately asked. Monks asked if he could come in. Julie ushered him through to the kitchen. 'What do you know about this?' she asked him. 'Please don't lie to me,' she added as she passed him the note. Monks just looked at her, as she broke down crying. He then started to read the note. It only had a couple of lines saying: I have to leave, for reasons I cannot say. I'm so sorry, I never meant to hurt any of you. You will always be in my thoughts. Monks spoke in a soft voice, 'I don't know why or where he has gone.' Then he moved in close and held Julie in his arms in an attempt to try and comfort her as she sobbed out loud.

Mickey was standing in the corner looking dumbfounded next to Mr Kravis. Then Monks asked her, 'Have the police been here?' Julie composed herself and replied, 'Yes, asking where Luke is.' 'What did you say?' Monks asked. 'Nothing we don't know what's happened.' Mr Kravis was watching Monks with great care, as he couldn't be sure what Luke's best mate was actually up to.

It had seemed to take an age, but Luke had finally arrived at Istanbul's mainline station. This was the part he was keen on experiencing. Obviously Luke would have liked to visit this diverse city where Europe meets Asia in different circumstances, but he was planning on making the most of his short stay before the next tiring leg of his course. It did not take long to navigate his way out of the station and hail a taxi, in which an excitable young Turk read Luke's details on where he would be hoping to stay. Then, in broken English, on the short ride he began offering Luke a wide range of activities and substances, which Luke politely declined to take him up on. When they pulled up to the three-star Yusufpasa Konagi hotel right in the heart of the city Luke gave the taxi driver a few lira and told him to keep the change. The man helped Luke with his luggage and handed Luke his card with his phone details on it, reminding Luke once more that he would provide him with whatever he needed. Luke smiled and agreed that he would be in touch if he did need anything. Walking into the lobby and up to reception Luke was impressed with the way the hotel was designed. He assumed that it was in the Ottoman Empire Turkish style. The cool air-conditioning felt good after the heat of the taxi ride. Luke had found the heat outside overwhelming, which was unusual for this time of year. He waited at the reception desk briefly before an attractive middle-aged woman greeted him. She informed him that there was room available at a very reasonable rate, which Luke agreed to pay.

Monks received the obligatory visit from the Metropolitan Police. He behaved as ever when dealing with the Old Bill – with a calm demeanour and politeness. You would not believe that this was the same short-tempered, violent thug these officers knew him to be. They did not want to arrest him, they explained, they had just come round to make some enquires. Obviously, they asked if he had any knowledge of the recent goings-on around the manor. Monks feigned complete surprise at the information that they had just given him. When the two detectives moved the subject on to the key suspect and his possible whereabouts Monks genuinely did not know a thing, as he had no idea where his best friend Luke had gone (though even if he had, he would never tell the police). The more experienced of the two officers soon realised that Monks had no knowledge of recent events and left Monks alone with a warning that they had not finished with him yet and may have to call on him again. Monks smiled at the officers and walked to the door with them. 'I am always happy to be of assistance,' He said and sneered at the officers. They did not bother to reply.

Monks waited for the police to get out of sight before heading over to see Luke's Uncle Darren. On the way back he thought it might be a good idea to have a chat with the old man. He remembered that Luke was always banging on about him. Maybe he knows something I don't, he mused.

After a fine night's sleep, Luke awoke to the Muslim call to prayer that was sounding across the city. He stretched out and yawned. He felt completely refreshed after his long trek across Europe. Now he was keen to get up, explore the city and chill out for a couple of days before the gruelling journey that lay ahead of him. Luke walked out into Istanbul where the temperature was cooler and much more seasonal for October. Making sure he had plenty of Turkish lira he began strolling through the busy streets. The first thing that struck him was the mixture of the old and the new. He noticed a brash glass hotel that seemed to creep up behind historic old buildings. There were women walking along dressed from head to toe in Western designer clothes, passing other women in long skirts and Islamic head coverings; such a contrast. He soon found that he was next to the Bosphorus, stretched out in all its glory in front of him. Turning another corner, he stood right in front of Taksim Station where he had arrived the day before. Feeling peckish as he passed a traditional Turkish restaurant he thought he would like to eat what the locals eat, and entered the lively restaurant-cum-bar, which had a cool, clean Turkish feel.

After the two days he spent exploring and discovering all the glorious sights and sounds of the city, he felt that he had experienced the real Istanbul. Luke had begun to unwind and prepare for the trials and tribulations that might lie ahead. He had a hot soapy shower before he left his hotel as he could not be sure when he would be able to enjoy another one. Then he packed all of his gear up and took a cab to Taksim Station. Arriving there it did not take him long to board the 8 a.m. train to Aleppo.

As he settled into his seat on the Toros Express, he checked his rucksack to see that he had plenty of water and food, as this train had no buffet car. The scenery soon became all too familiar. Constantly passing by were endless olive groves and pistachio trees, broken every now and then by herds of cattle. As the Toros Express, which was surprisingly comfortable, snaked its way through the Turkish countryside he looked at the information that he had written down, noticing that this part of the journey would take up to thirty-five hours. He closed his eyes and then all the events of the past couple of weeks started to replay in his mind. It was too much time to go over all that had happened to him in what had felt like no time at all.

Luke woke as the train made its final few shunts into Aleppo. He was feeling quite chilled out – he had managed to sleep remarkably well once he finally stopped thinking about London. Now he had perked up and was ready for the next leg. Luke stepped down off the train. He would readily admit he was feeling slightly wary now that he was venturing out of Europe into the Middle East. He pushed his shoulders back and strode through the station as if he had lived there all his life, one of the locals returning home, even though it was obvious that he was a westerner. He soon realised that he would not be able to travel to Amman in Jordan until the next morning, so he would have to find a hotel to stay in for the night. This was not what he had planned to do but he sighed and thought that he would just have to make the best of it. He quickly found a busy souk and casually wandered through. Eventually he came across an ancient thirteenth-century mosque, where a kindly old man shared an aniseed tasting drink with him and in broken English directed him to some accommodation. Luke did not understand when the man tried to explain the name of the local brew, but he was extremely grateful for his generosity and for his help in finding him a bed in what was a strange, but to his surprise, welcoming land.

Shannon, in the meantime, had settled back in Sydney as if she had never been away. Her trusted childhood friend Debbie had met her at the airport and she moved in with her, hopefully just for a week or so. It was great to see her dear friend again. She could confide in her with no fear of disappointment or indeed, more importantly, judgement. Debbie shared her tidy home with her only sibling, which was one more than Shannon had. She said that Shannon could stay as long as she liked, though Shannon promised that it would only be until she found her feet and organised some accommodation for when Luke arrived in a week or maybe two. Shannon soon began to adjust to conditions and she felt safe away from the nightmare she had stumbled blindly into in a dark corner of Soho back in London's glamorous West End.

21

Disposing of the Evidence

Sydney

As they drove across the city, Harwood was still thinking about Kerry. He liked her. Milo switched off his mobile and then reminded him of the matter in hand.

'Let's cut this bastard up quickly,' he said, then proceeded to turn on the police siren. Harwood was not looking forward to the gruesome assignment that awaited them. They raced back to the police station in double-quick time. No matter how many times you have to do it, you cannot get used to or enjoy cutting up a corpse. It is a time-consuming process and the smell of a rotting body is an odour that will take days to get out of your nostrils. They knew from experience that if you left a corpse in the huge deep freezer that Milo kept in his 'abattoir' for a week or two, in this case three, the decaying process would stop temporarily, and makes the frozen flesh slightly easier to chop into smaller pieces. They would have to get a move on though, because as soon as the flesh starts to defrost the awful stench quickly returns. This would be the fifth body of which they'd had to dispose. Over three weeks had passed and by now Jay Edwards's regular punters would know that he had gone missing, without having a clue as to where he had gone.

On finishing their shift, Harwood followed Milo out to his

motor for the drive up to his suburban hideaway, where they had set out a special area in which to perform their grisly act. Nobody passing by Milo's home would ever be any the wiser of the goings-on in there, as everything seemed in keeping with a typical house in the suburbs.

Before they began their work there was always an uneasy silence between them. It wasn't clear whether this was a sign that they knew what they were doing was wrong or if it was because not speaking about the truth meant it somehow didn't seem real. Arriving at Milo's home they parked close to the garage and got out of the car. Milo waved at his elderly neighbour, who had always felt so safe living next door to a law-abiding police officer. Milo smirked at this ludicrous image. He got quite a kick out of the fact that nobody realised what he was really like. As for Harwood, he knew that he was now in far too deep to stop these macabre goings-on. So he reluctantly waved at Milo's pleasant neighbour as they made their route into the cold dark cellar, where a three-week-old frozen solid Jay Edwards was waiting to be dismembered into tiny little pieces then scattered all over various parts of New South Wales.

On entering Milo's eerie cellar-cum-abattoir Harwood saw all sorts of by now familiar, horrific-looking tools scattered around the place. There were butcher's saws, knives, surgeon's tools and three or four contraptions that even Milo did not know the function of. Jay's frozen corpse was lifted out of the deep freeze and dropped down onto the large slab right next to it. They had already begun slicing up the body. They had removed both hands and feet the previous night and placed them in four separate ziplock plastic bags and positioned them one on top of the other in the corner of the cellar. This afternoon they were about to remove the legs past the knees and the arms from above the elbows. Milo looked the corpse up and down for a minute, sighed, then went to put on the protective plastic suit so none of the blood or other various bodily fluids would be able to touch his own skin. Harwood followed the exact same procedure. Then they selected an assortment of saws, knives and cleavers. One of them stood at each end of the corpse and the grisly work began.

Raising his meat cleaver high up into the air, Milo aimed and brought the cleaver down hard above the elbow, almost severing the arm completely. Thick congealed blood stained the slab. Milo wiped some of the remaining sinew off his cleaver all across his plastic suit, covering his midriff. 'Dirty bastard,' he said, laughing aloud. He actually enjoyed cutting up bodies. Harwood followed suit, and began hacking away just above the left knee. He, however, did not feel quite as enthusiastic about their depressing task. This was a tough job; it would take a while to get it finished.

Two hours later, Harwood and Milo had nearly finished. The legs were cut off up to the knee, and then another section from above the knee to the waist was cut off and removed. Harwood then placed the pieces into four separate black bags, which they tied up with string and placed over in the corner of the cellar with the other limbs. The same happened with the arms – two sections from the wrist to the elbow and from the elbow to the shoulder. If anyone were able to see the carcass they would have presumed it was a butcher's fine cut of meat. They had both inadvertently become masters in the art of butchering. Not a lot of Jay Edwards's body remained to chop up. Milo stopped to wipe sweat and specks of blood from his brow and asked Harwood, 'Do you want to cut off his head?' Harwood could not comprehend the casual tone Milo adopted as he offered him the task. 'No, mate, I'll leave that to you.'

'Good, this is my favourite part of the job.' What a sick bastard, thought Harwood. Milo then went across to his tool selection and picked up a heavy-duty hammer.

He tapped it on his wooden bench to test its suitability

then walked back over to the remains of the chopped-up dealer and proceeded to smash all of the teeth out of Jay's mouth, to destroy any dental evidence. Harwood surveyed the carnage that lay around them and threw up. He promised himself that this would be the final time that he would take part in this awful procedure, as the rancid smell made him throw up for the second time. Milo went back over to his ghoulish collection of apparatus and selected a medium-sized axe. Harwood decided that he had done enough and decided to start cleaning the floor of the cellar. He picked up a hard broom and swept away all of the excess congealed blood and guts and sinew. He chose not to watch as Milo took two steps back, then swung the axe around before bringing it down onto the neck. He instantly separated the head from the shoulders at the very first attempt. The head rolled off the slab onto the ground with a dull thud. Just at that moment Harwood turned around and was met with the hideous sight of Jay's head lying on the floor with both of his eyes wide open. They seemed to stare directly at him. Harwood could not look away. Then he began to vomit yet again.

Watching his colleague throw up, Milo thought that now might be the time to arrange for the young English chap, who one of his contacts overseas had put in touch with him a few months ago, to repay his debt. He had been recommended as someone capable of carrying out a hit for them, but Milo and Harwood had decided to sort that particular problem out themselves. Therefore they carried it out and had decided to put the young man on standby. What was his name? thought Milo. Oh, it'll come to me, he has a past he needs to keep quiet, plus the fact he now owes them big-time. Just to help us out now, so his colleague Harwood could live a normal life if only for a little while.

22

The End of the Line

England

Waking up in Aleppo, Luke, not for the first time on his route, was feeling apprehensive about what the next twenty-four hours might hold. After showering, he quickly prepared everything and made his way out of the small room he had slept in. As he was leaving, the owner of the premises wished Luke a safe journey and said that he hoped that God would take care of him. Another nice gesture from these warm people, Luke thought, as he waved at the proprietor and went on his way. He soon returned to the train station and navigated his way to the bus that he had to board to travel across to Jordan. Only a handful of other travellers were on this service. The dusty old bus was soon leaving the station. The trip to the border would take around five hours, maybe more.

As the bus came to a stop near the border, the driver began talking to the passengers in Arabic. Luke did not understand what had been said and was grateful when one of the other passengers informed him in good English that he would be required to obtain a visa to cross the border into Jordan. They all got off the bus and the driver directed them towards customs. Waiting for almost an hour, Luke kept looking at his passport while the customs officers carefully checked everyone's documents. When it came to Luke's turn, he could not help but start to feel anxious. He need not have worried as the immigration officer barely gave him a second look. Luke paid the fee of about £11, and then Luke was waved on through with no hassle whatsoever. Luke was stunned at the ease of the whole procedure. He had imagined it would be a lot of bother travelling through this unpredictable part of the world, but so far so good, he thought. Maybe getting into Israel would be more of an ordeal. First, though, he had to board yet another bus to move him down to the Allenby Bridge, where security would take on a completely new meaning.

Uncle Darren had brought in the morning papers and switched on the lights in the back room of the shop. To his surprise, there were two men waiting for him there. He stood there frozen to the spot, his mind yelling at him to run. Opposite him he could make out the figure of a stocky, pug-faced man who looked like he had lost more fights than he had won. Behind him stood the late Danny Chilton's driver, Rixon. Darren knew why they were there. Everybody in the underworld seemed to have heard the rumours about Danny's so-called assassin. 'Where is he?' one of them blurted out. Darren did not bother to answer. What would be the point? They weren't going to believe that he had no idea where his favourite nephew had gone. The pug-faced man approached Darren. As he moved in closer, Darren could not help but think what an ugly bastard this man was. He knew what was coming, though. Darren was no simpleton. In his youth he had run with a fearsome mob of football hooligans. The man had experienced a few battles in his time. On a few occasions in the past he had aided Rixon out of some nasty moments, but that almost certainly wasn't going to help him now. He realised at this point that he was in serious trouble. Even if he could tell them anything, he wouldn't. He just had to take whatever they were going to do and pray that they did not kill him.

'Come on, Darren, do yourself a favour,' said Rixon.

'I can't help you.'

Rixon sighed. 'Go on then.'

Pug then delivered a searing right-handed blow across Darren's jaw. Darren stumbled backwards, crashed into the door frame leading to the kitchen and fell to the floor.

Just then, a customer entered the shop. Rixon went over to the customer and said, 'We're closed, come back later.' The customer sharply turned on his heel and was gone. Rixon then bolted the shop door closed. Pug laughed as he stood over Darren, who could not feel his jaw. He reached down and picked Darren up and then threw him across the room. This was no mean feat, as Darren was a big lad. He felt himself slam into the opposite wall then he seemed to slide down into a heap on the deck. Moving around he saw the ugly bastard staring at him, like a Rottweiler waiting for the command from its owner to attack. Rixon came across and cracked his knuckles. Warm blood filled Darren's mouth and he spat out a volley of blood, which landed near to Pug's feet.

'Darren, we go back a long way,' said Rixon.

Yeah, thought Darren, and I've bailed you out of the shit many times.

'Do the right thing and tell us.'

Darren stared up at pug-faced man and then looked at Rixon. In my youth, I would have kicked the Christ out of the pair of you, he said to himself. Still, he had chosen not to say a word to these two thugs. He smiled through gritted teeth and stuck up his middle finger, then with an almighty surge pulled himself up to try to wrestle with Pug.

He pushed Pug into the door frame, who then clattered into Rixon. Darren took three steps back as he watched the two before him rolling around on the floor. Darren leapt on top of Pug and punched him twice hard on his already flat nose. Blood squirted across the lino. Rixon cracked his knuckles again. He had to get this sorted before Darren gained the upper hand. He pulled the cosh from the back of his trousers and steamed into Darren with such force the cosh nearly broke in two. Darren remained bolt upright on top of Pug, his arms dropping to his sides. Then, he slowly fell to one side. Pug pushed him off and rose to his feet, wiping the blood off his splattered nose. He looked down at Darren lying flat on the ground, then looked at Rixon, who was puffing and panting after the exertion of bashing Darren's head in with the cosh. Pug grabbed the cosh and began to pound Darren's head in some more. 'Leave him, that's enough,' said Rixon, pulling him away. Pug pulled all the newspapers into the room and piled them up around Darren on the floor, along with boxes and anything else that would catch fire easily. Rixon stood there watching as the room was filled with flammable material.

Pug carefully began sealing off the room so no air could escape. When he was finished, Rixon looked down at Darren, who might well have been dead as he was not moving at all.

'Come on, we have to go,' Pug shouted at Rixon, who was staring at Darren still. Pug lit a match and threw it onto the kindling.

'You mug, Darren, why didn't you tell me?' Rixon said as he felt a tinge of guilt for his old hooligan pal. He looked about at the flames quickly spreading around the room. They left by the back and Rixon closed the door behind him. They strode briskly back round to the front of the shop and in a cavalier fashion pulled the metal shutter down. Calmly walking onto the high street, they stopped to take a quick glance around; nobody was taking a blind bit of notice as they wandered a few short steps up the street, opened up their car door, jumped in and drove away.

The choking thick and black smoke was already swallowing up the entire atmosphere inside the shop. Darren came to and let out a huge gasp of air. He was confused, as he could not see in front of him. Coughing and spluttering, he quickly came to realise that this could well be the end. He had to stay close to the ground.

Luke was now keyed up for what he hoped would be the short trip down to the Allenby terminal in Jordan and then on to Jerusalem. In addition, he was relishing the thought of meeting up with his old girlfriend, Lindsay, and the fact that she now worked for the Israeli secret service had him completely intrigued. What an incredible thing for that shy little girl he remembered from Shepherd's Bush Green to be doing. He was spot on; the trip did not take very long. He was wandering around the terminal looking at the Allenby Bridge. Luke's information was that this was the easiest point of entry into Israel, and at this crossing they would not put a stamp on your passport when exiting Jordan. Luke's theory was that this meant there would be no proof that he had ever left Jordan. Perhaps this may fool the police, immigration and whoever else, were now on his trail. He presumed that the trail would go cold at some point in the Middle East. Ingenious thinking, Luke surmised, or so he had to believe.

As he edged nearer to passport control on the bridge he could feel his stomach turning over yet again. All he had to do now was remain calm and show his identification to the security immigration police. He showed a sallow-looking man his papers; the man took a brief look then hurried him through onto another waiting bus.

He took a seat on the vehicle and watched as it soon began to fill up with a full complement of Arab passengers. He sensed a different atmosphere altogether for the first time. Watching anxiously as they crossed the Allenby Bridge, Luke was stunned as he looked out at the great River Jordan. He knew a great deal of biblical history, as his mother had sent both him and his brother to Sunday school regularly when they were children. He thought that it resembled the Great Trickle of Jordan – it was hardly a stream, let alone a river. Where was it? His shock at the second-rate sight was soon forgotten as the scenery changed once again.

As they entered the State of Israel under a huge Star of David flag, it felt as if he had just landed on a different planet. They were stopping at many separate checkpoints. Soldiers were milling about carrying M16 machine guns and looking as if they were ready to use them at any given moment. There was an air of mistrust as the bus stopped suddenly and the military boarded, demanding to see identification. Then, an austere grizzled-looking senior officer got on and told everyone to leave the vehicle immediately. Luke disembarked to witness what he could only describe as absolute mayhem. People were queuing up for what looked like a mile at least. All around there were buses parked up with hundreds of people walking in the same direction. Israelis standing behind metal barriers moved the surging crowds forward towards what Luke presumed was immigration.

As they approached customs a surly young soldier was collecting up entire loads of luggage and taking them away to be X-rayed. Fair enough, Luke thought. They had to be extra vigilant in this part of the world as all of their Arab neighbours seemed to want to wipe the Israeli state off the map. His mood started to change and he became concerned as he stood around not moving anywhere for nearly an hour. Finally, he found himself in front of the immigration desk. An unsympathetic-looking woman greeted him. 'PASSPORT,' she barked at him. Charming, he felt like saying, but he chose to bite his lip. She seemed to gape at his passport for an age and then looked him up and down a couple of times, then stared at the passport some more. She stared directly at him again and then asked, 'Why have you come here?' Luke turned on the old Crooks charm. Smiling at her he said, 'I want to visit the Holy Land.'

'How long do you intend to stay?' she asked, then blankly waited for Luke to reply.

He smiled at her politely. 'A week or so, maybe, then I will move on to Lebanon.'

Why he had told her that nugget of information, he had absolutely no idea. She stared at him for a little longer. Luke felt apprehensive as she kept on staring, and then all of a sudden, without another word, she handed him back his passport unstamped and then nodded at him to walk on through. He walked through the terminal only to spend another half an hour looking for his bags amongst the masses of other luggage piled up all over the place. Feeling relieved, he checked that no one was watching him and left the terminal to find a taxi to take him into Jerusalem.

It did not take any time at all to find a cab – there were literally stacks of them, all lined up in an orderly fashion. Luke could not tell if his driver was Israeli or Palestinian – not that it mattered to him anyway, he was just curious, but he decided not to ask. 'Where are you going, my friend?' he asked. Luke took out a piece of notepaper that he had carefully folded in half when Mr Kravis gave it to him. It was the address of a comfortable hotel named the Jerusalem Gate at 43 Yirmiyahu Street. 'Yes, my friend, we will soon be there,' he confirmed, then drove away off towards the city. Soon the taxi driver began pointing out various landmarks to Luke on the way, explaining that one way led to the Dead Sea and the other to Jericho. All very interesting, but Luke was not really listening. He was tired after hours on a coach and hanging around at border control. He perked up, though, as in front of him he saw the golden dome gleaming in the sun as they passed the Damascus Gate on the north side of the old city.

*　　*　　*

Julie had just finished her rounds. She only had a few of the old girls left in and around the estate on her client list these days, whose hair she cut, coloured and permed regularly. Slowly but surely they were all dying off and she did not want to take on any more new clients as she had to take a great deal more care of Mickey for now. She did not like to leave Mickey on his own all day, although he did have a terrific club that he attended every morning to keep him occupied while his mother was at work. She sometimes felt a sense of guilt leaving him there for long periods and preferred to pick him up at around lunchtime. These feelings had intensified since Luke had not been about for over a week now, as he would usually help where he could. She buckled up in her sporty Peugeot 205 then drove off to the wholesalers before picking Mickey up.

Julie was not in the store for more than ten minutes, but as she went back to her car she was positive that she saw a familiar-looking man who she had noticed on two, or maybe three, separate occasions in the last week. Was he following her? Julie put it down to her imagination as she had already spoken to the police twice. She was still just a little perplexed about recent events. Julie was positive that she saw the familiar figure again as she neared the community centre. It was strange she thought that the figure looked very similar to Monks. Don't be daft, Julie said in her head. Thinking no more of it she parked up and went inside to collect her boy.

The Jerusalem Gate Hotel lobby was elegant. I could soon get used to this, Luke thought, as he collected his room key and made his way to the elevators. He had time for a nice sleep and a hot shower and then he would have to meet Lindsay at 8 p.m. at the lobby bar. He was looking forward to seeing her for the first time in more than six years. Time seemed to fly past. It was almost half past seven when he leapt out of bed to get ready in time. He checked his hair before leaving his hotel room and felt his stomach roll over as he washed the putty out of his hands. 'Let's do this, Luke,' he said as he splashed on a touch more aftershave. Grabbing his room key, he turned off the lights and headed for the lobby. He nodded at the concierge as he stepped out of the lift and then walked into the elegant lobby bar.

As Lindsay had left her office to get to the hotel she had wondered what her old boyfriend would look like now. They were so close when they grew up together, they shared a lot of laughs back then. How had he gotten himself into so much trouble? Still, Luke will tell all before long, she thought. She was pleased that she may be the one to help get Luke out of the angst he had managed to find himself in. Lindsay was already sitting in the corner of the room scanning who was coming in and out of the place when Luke took a seat at the bar. He was observing everyone in there as it was quite busy at this time. The bartender asked what he would like to drink. He ordered a small beer, and then a voice behind him said, 'Well, fancy seeing you here.' Luke's heart skipped a beat. He composed himself, then turned around to face his first true love. 'Lindsay, it's been a while.' Then they smiled at each other and embraced, hugging each other tightly; it was an emotional moment for the two of them. After a long clinch, they gradually loosened their grip on each other. Lindsay stepped back to take a good look at Luke as he did her. Both were speechless for a moment until the bartender piped up and asked if Lindsay would be requiring a drink at all. 'No, thank you,' she replied and then she touched Luke on the waist and asked him, 'So why are you here?' Luke sighed and held onto her hand as he began to explain the difficult situation, even though they both knew that her grandfather had already filled her in with all the details.

After an hour Lindsay excused herself, as she had to

answer a phone call. Luke watched her with interest as she looked away from him and began speaking in fluent Yiddish. Fantastic, he thought as she flicked her long brunette hair from her brown eyes. He forgot all about Shannon for a moment and the reason why he was here. When Lindsay finished her phone call she suggested that they go out and relax for the rest of the evening in a lively part of town, for old time's sake. Luke agreed, as Lindsay had already stated that she was able to sort out all the identification and required visa as soon as possible for him. But in return for all of that, he would owe the people she works for a debt, which she would reveal to him later. He had realised that he would need to give them something in return for their assistance, but it didn't worry him. After all, it wasn't as if they would want him to kill someone for them.

'Come on, the car is here,' Lindsay told him.

'That was quick.' Lindsay smiled at him and then stood up. Luke followed her out to the waiting vehicle.

As Julie turned the corner into their road, she kept an eye on the rear-view mirror, pleased that the familiar car behind them was no longer pursuing them. Mickey asked if she was okay. 'Of course, sweetheart,' she replied. She felt relieved to be so close to home. When they pulled up outside their house she looked across at Mr Kravis's place and noticed that his curtains were still drawn, which was quite unusual as it was well past lunchtime. She turned off the engine and stepped out of the car and Mickey followed. Julie glanced at Mr Kravis's window again and decided to get Mickey settled indoors then pop over to check that everything was okay. Something came over her and she shivered as if someone had just walked over her grave as she approached her front door and took out her keys. She closed the door behind them and they both went into the kitchen. Julie and Mickey both gasped when they saw the kitchen door hanging off its hinges. 'Stay right here,' she said. Mickey stood dead still, not quite sure what had happened. Julie ran upstairs to see what the burglars had stolen. To her surprise, nothing looked out of place. By now Julie was not frightened, although she was confused. Why break in and not steal anything? It didn't make any sense, she thought. After checking all of the bedrooms she went back downstairs. As she ventured back into the kitchen she said to Mickey, 'Nothing has been taken, sweetheart.'

Julie froze when she saw her son tied to a chair and blindfolded, with a gag in his mouth. A tall menacing muscular figure who was dressed all in black stood there. His face was almost covered completely except for the eyes and mouth in a black balaclava. He was holding a large hunting knife to Mickey's throat. Then, in the reflection of the glass in the kitchen window, she saw standing directly behind her the familiar outline of the man she thought she had seen many times recently – it couldn't be Monks here to save them, could it? Before she could react, he moved smartly in front of her and viciously punched her to the floor. She came round dazed and confused. She could not see, it was black as night – they had blindfolded and gagged her. A pain came shooting through her head from the blow that had decked her. Slowly the man removed the blindfold and spoke to her. 'Do not make a sound, okay?' Julie nodded as he started to loosen the gag. She looked directly at Mickey. He seemed like he was as calm as he could be in a situation like this. The familiar-looking man, also in a balaclava, was staring directly at her. This was not a good sign, Julie realised. She had to try to remain focused on getting out of here as fast as possible.

'All we want is to know is where he is.'

Of course, she knew who they were talking about, but she honestly didn't know where he was, hence the obvious answer: 'I don't know, he just left.'

The tall black-clad man remained silent.

'One more chance, darling,' said the other man.

'I told you, I don't know.'

He sighed and then looked at his muscular associate. 'Turn the iron on.'

Julie repeated to them, 'I don't know, I am telling the truth.'

She was starting to cry and blubber. She had an inkling about what they were intending to do as the iron began to steam. The black-clad man picked up the iron, spat on it and then watched it hiss and steam. He walked across to her, iron in hand, while the familiar figure ripped open her blouse and then her bra to leave her bare breasts exposed in front of them. He took the iron from his associate then said, 'Come on, make it easy for you and the boy.'

'No, you bastards, I don't know!' She pushed herself forward and spat towards the pair of them. They both began to laugh. She had heard that laugh before. It can't be, she thought and then he pushed the iron to within an inch of her breasts. She could feel the intense heat and steam near to her skin. She gritted her teeth, trying to prepare herself for the unbearable searing pain.

'Hang on a minute,' the familiar-looking man said as Julie was crying and spitting all down her chin. 'Let's warm the boy up, then she'll talk.' She was sure he was trying to disguise his voice.

It took a second for what they had just said to register.

'No, please, no – not Mickey.'

They both went over to Mickey who remained perfectly still throughout the ordeal so far. Julie became hysterical. She had to protect her little boy somehow.

The car pulled away from the hotel. Luke sat in the back with Lindsay. She commented again on how good it was to catch up, but in what strange circumstances. Luke nodded in agreement. And then Lindsay's tone changed. She suddenly became much more serious.

'We will have everything you need by the end of the week,' she said. He was listening intently, waiting for the catch. Lindsay tapped on the blacked-out glass separating them from the driver. The shield opened and a brown package appeared. She took it and slit open the top, taking out the documents inside. She handed Luke an A4-sized photograph of what looked like a mid-thirtyish, white European male. What the fuck is she showing me this for? was all he could think. She then proceeded to read out all the details of who he was and where he resided in Australia. Luke's stomach began to turn over as he came to realise what the 'favour' for their assistance in creating his new identity would be. Luke was completely dumbfounded by what they were asking of him. He asked for a little time to consider their offer. Lindsay tapped on the screen and began speaking in Yiddish. After a short conversation, the screen closed shut.

'You can decline our offer. You have until tomorrow to decide.'

Luke was shell-shocked by what she had just asked him to do. Could this be the same innocent little girl that he used to play with and had a crush on back in Shepherd's Bush not so long ago?

The car came to a halt and Lindsay opened the door. The noise surrounded them as they stepped out into the German colony south-east of the city centre. Luke stood still for a second. His head was spinning from the shock of what his part of the arrangement would be. Lindsay held out for his hand. 'Come on, let's go have some fun,' she said. Fun? Luke thought. You've just asked me to murder someone for you and now we are going to party all night. He couldn't believe the situation he was in. How could she switch from 'Oh, by the way, can you skip off and execute this man for me?' to 'Let's go and get wrecked' thirty seconds later. He had to try to get his head around this as they walked past the lively restaurants. He could hear everyone chatting in English rather than Hebrew. *'Anglos'* was the local term.

Luke needed a drink; in fact, he needed a few drinks. Lindsay stopped outside the Izen bar, which was pumping out loud drum and bass music. It was a popular place as all the local DJs played there. 'Here we are, Luke, come.' She went straight to the front of the young crowd queuing to get in. Luke walked with her, not saying a word. The security staff moved to one side to let them both in, all of them smiling and laughing with Lindsay. They went through to a large outdoor area. It was not quite as busy as the inside of the bar. She took them over to a quiet corner where they could hear each other speak. Luke had now relaxed a touch. His head was adapting to the sounds of the DJ as the 'favour' these people wished him to carry out began to sink in. Lindsay moved in close and spoke softly to him, 'I want you tonight.' Then she kissed him gently on the mouth. Luke responded to her soft lips. In that moment, all his thoughts of Shannon disappeared as they kissed passionately.

Mickey stayed absolutely still as the blindfold was removed. The gag was still shoved tight in his mouth so that he could not make a sound. The tall black-clad man pulled Mickey's head backwards and held the iron above his forehead. Julie, by now completely hysterical, yelled out for them to leave him alone. The tall black-clad man put the iron on the worktop next to Mickey and went to whisper something to his associate. They both looked at Julie and then at Mickey.

'Just tell us where he is, and then nobody is going to get hurt.'

Julie took a gulp of air and tried to compose herself. They gave her a moment to try to calm down. Eventually she managed to catch her breath.

'Listen to me, Luke has gone away and we don't know where.'

The two men stood in silence for an instant. Then the familiar one knelt down by the side of Julie and touched her naked breasts. Mickey began to get irate at this scene and started to move violently in his chair to the amusement of them both.

'Stay calm, sweetheart,' she said to Mickey through gritted teeth.'

'Nice and firm, darling, I could have some fun with these,' he whispered to her threateningly.

Just outside the gate that led into his sister's back garden stood Darren, coughing and spluttering, his lungs full of the thick black smoke. He had somehow managed to kick his way out of his shop and escape shortly before the fire brigade had arrived to put out the fire. Realising that the Chilton mob would be paying Julie a visit he had tried to warn her before they got to her. As she was not answering her mobile phone he'd feared the worst. He had stopped off at his house to pick up some essentials. He hoped that he could get Julie and Mickey out of danger before the evil bastards that Jack had sent inflicted any needless pain on them.

Darren peeked through the kitchen door. He could see Julie sitting there with the perverted yob standing in front of her, humiliating her in front of his nephew. He was infuriated, but he knew that he had to stay calm and strike at the right time or they could all end up dead. The tall black-clad man picked up the iron again and started to come across to Julie. The familiar one, who had always had a thing for Julie, got bored with fondling her breasts, decided to up the ante and began moving his shovel-like hands in-between her thighs. Mickey was starting to go ballistic. He was bound tightly to the chair and it had tipped over so that he was lying on his side, trying to move across to his mother. The tall black-clad man looked around and laughed at his pathetic attempt to stop Julie's ongoing ordeal. Darren saw this as his chance. Taking the CS gas canister from his coat pocket he gripped it tightly and snuck in through the already beaten down back door.

Julie was looking straight through her kitchen directly at Darren. He carefully indicated to her to close her eyes. She could see that he had a pair of goggles covering his own eyes. With both of the men concentrating on Julie, Darren had a tiny window to step in front of Mickey without the two thugs noticing. He put his finger up to his lips to indicate for Mickey to remain silent as he cut the bindings that tied him to the chair with a Stanley knife. Darren grabbed Mickey firmly as he released him and pushed him towards the exit. Mickey realised that for his mother's sake he had to do exactly what his Uncle Darren had instructed him to do, even though he wanted to hurt those two animals who were abusing his mother.

The tall black-clad man stood there with the iron in his hand, watching while his associate began to take pleasure in tampering with Julie. Darren had the CS gas in his left hand and a claw hammer in the other. He crept right up behind them. Julie's eyes were closed and she was shaking as the humiliation continued. He stood directly behind them both, well within striking distance. Aiming the spray at the head of the bastard who was eagerly abusing Julie, he raised the claw hammer high ready to bring it down on the other's skull. 'You fucking bastards!' he shouted out. The tall black-clad man turned like a spring coil and launched at him with the iron, just clipping the top of Darren's forehead. Darren brought the claw hammer crashing down onto his nose. The CS gas canister flew across the kitchen floor, as did the two men from the heavy blows they had given each other. The familiar-looking thug began to panic as the two of them lay sparked out. He watched as the gas canister settled by the back door and saw that the boy had gone.

'Shit, you bitch,' he spat, then struck Julie, knocking the chair over with the force.

He walked across to where the gas canister lay, but before he could get anywhere near, Mickey ran through the door, armed with a cricket bat and swinging it wildly above his head. He ran at the man, screaming loudly at him. The thug was startled and took a couple of paces back. Mickey was still lashing out uncontrollably with the cricket bat but was getting nowhere near him, so the man simply waited for Mickey to run out of steam. He intended to kick the shit out of the childish lad he had known all his life.

While all this was playing out in front of him, Darren, groggy from the recent blow, his lungs still full of acrid smoke, was scarcely conscious. He somehow half rose to his feet and with a final surge of adrenalin managed to grab hold of the iron. He was still only just out of the bastard's vision, but close enough for one good hearty blow.

Across the road, Mr Kravis lay on his living room floor, gasping for air. He had crawled across to the telephone and just about managed to ring the police to inform them of what had happened. He only hoped that he was not too late. The two thugs had visited him first and had made a couple of threats. He had not revealed anything to them, but they did not believe him and had given him a severe beating just for the hell of it. He lay in wait for an ambulance.

Darren mustered up just enough strength and pounded the familiar thug on his ear. He heard an almighty crack as the thug crashed heavily to the floor. Darren felt his head spinning, then dropped down onto his knees; he could hear police sirens edging ever closer. As the familiar thug regained consciousness, he took off his balaclava and felt his ear warm with blood. He knew he had to be careful that Julie did not see his face. Mickey had seen him though and could not quite believe it. He turned away and was holding tight onto his mother. They were both crying and comforting each other.

Quietly and very slowly the familiar thug sneaked out of the back door and jumped the wall in the garden, managing to avoid the police narrowly as four heavy-duty coppers steamed through the back gate at that precise moment.

At the same time the ambulance had arrived to give assistance to Mr Kravis. As the paramedics wheeled him out to the waiting vehicle, he could see the police and further paramedics rushing in and out of Julie's house. He was so short of breath by this stage he could hardly speak to the young man attending to him. He tried to ask how his friends were but by now his voice had become barely audible, so the young paramedic failed to understand what the extremely concerned but incredibly weak old man was trying to ask him.

The next day Luke woke up in his hotel room in Jerusalem after a night of deep passion. Rubbing the sleep out of his eyes he turned to see that Lindsay had gone. She had left a note on the pillow next to him, with the name Andy Karacan and another photograph of the man they wished for him to visit. Written in large capital letters were the words 'MEET ME TONIGHT AT THE IZEN BAR AT EIGHT'. Luke sat up and studied the details of the task. He wanted to go home. Was this what he was to become, an assassin? His head was fuzzy; he tried to go back to sleep and hoped that all of this was just a bad dream.

Three days later, after yet another visit from the doctor, Julie knew that they were only making sure that she was well enough to leave the hospital. Julie was pleased that, apart from a few cuts and bruises here and there, fortunately there was no permanent damage; well, physically, anyway. A much older doctor had taken over the rounds and seemed much more on the ball than the younger man who had attended to her up until last night. Frankly, she felt that he looked as if he needed some time off, as he seemed in a slumber most of the time when speaking to Julie and the other patients on her ward. The older doctor had recommended that she discharge from the hospital without further delay. She thanked him and was relieved to be able to get out of the hospital as soon as possible.

Julie packed all her things up. Before she left she went to see her badly beaten and burned hero brother, Darren. She decided to go to the intensive care ward with her boy Mickey, who had sat waiting patiently by his mother's bedside almost constantly. They wished to see how the unfortunate Mr Kravis was doing. He did not look very well; the poor man was lying still in a coma wired up to a life support machine. She leant over the kindly old man who had helped the Crooks family so often, kissed him gently on the forehead and whispered 'thank you' in his ear. She knew that without all the old man's help Luke would probably be dead, and for that, she would be eternally grateful.

Jack Chilton waited in a police cell at Paddington Green. He had not said a word to anyone except his trusted crooked solicitor, who had confidently told Jack he would easily have these charges dropped in no time at all. Jack was sitting down on his bunk, plotting on how to catch up with Luke Crooks and avenge his brother someday.

Monks was sipping a lager in the pub with the boys, laughing and joking, thinking that Jack and his mob would soon have him working with them. He had gotten away with it, he was one hundred percent sure that he had, as he rubbed his sore and badly swollen ear.

Over in Jerusalem, Luke stood admiring the Wailing Wall, transfixed by the large crowds as they prayed. He felt as if somehow he should be there, as if he had answered a kind of calling. He waited for a while, taking in the surreal scene, until he saw a space slowly appear. He took out the folded piece of paper from his pocket and walked up to find an area where he felt comfortable, where he could sense his message would belong. He looked around at all the people before finally choosing a spot he thought suitable to put his confession into the wall.

He had sat up late the night before and written all of his sins down. He wanted a fresh start, to begin again from this point. He stood for a moment, then pushed his small note of confession into the sacred wall and hoped that God would see his letter and be able to forgive him. Lindsay had followed him. As he turned away, Lindsay held onto his hand and smiled. He wiped away a tear from his eye and then he breathed in deeply as they walked along together to the waiting car.

Luke sat in the limousine without making a sound as the car made its journey out of Jerusalem. Lindsay still held his hand tightly. He gazed at her as all kinds of thoughts raced through his mind. He thought of his family, dear old Mr Kravis and of course his best friend, Monks, hoping that they would all be safe at home. They both remained silent on the journey to Tel Aviv airport. As they neared the airport, Luke looked at Lindsay and she smiled at him. Still no words were spoken. The car pulled up directly outside the Departures terminal. Lindsay moved closer to him and whispered into his ear, 'You are going to be fine, trust me.' Luke embraced her tightly. The moment seemed to last an eternity. As they let go she handed him his passport, tickets and all the other important details for the flight.

He had gone over all the details, logged the necessary numbers of his contact in Australia and agreed to honour their request. He checked the name of the man he was to meet when he arrived with her. 'Mills, is that right?' Luke asked. 'That's correct. Nathan Mills, he will help you to settle in,' she answered. He said goodbye and took a last look at Lindsay, the once innocent child who he played and grew up with a long time ago. Then he opened the door and stepped out of the vehicle. A hardened-looking official handed Luke his luggage. He thanked him then went straight into the building. Luke did not look back; he kept on walking forwards as his thoughts turned to Shannon. He was sorry that he had betrayed her by sleeping with Lindsay, but he could not help his feelings for his first love. He buried what had taken place with her at the back of his mind as he fixed his thoughts on Shannon. He couldn't wait to see her again. Luke walked through the sliding doors and looked up at the departures board to find the check-in desk. When he'd navigated his way to the desk there was only a small queue. Almost immediately he was at the front of the line. He smiled civilly at the middle-aged woman sitting at the counter. She checked his tickets and asked him to make his way towards the departure gate. He had no fear, it was a breeze.

Soon, he would be with Shannon away from all the mayhem. All he had to do now was to accept the fact of what he had done and, more to the point, what he had to do before he could settle into his new life in Sydney. Luke Crooks had become something he never would have dreamed of only a short time ago.

While drinking in the West End Monks met up with his new pal Rixon. He shared a beer and a laugh with him and then went to Jack Chilton's home. After a night of drinking and deep conversation he agreed to take Jack up on his generous offer. After all, what choice did he have? In the early hours, Monks stood up to leave. Jack told Rixon to give Monks a ride home. As they shook hands, Jack said to him, 'Let me know when you find him.' Monks nodded then left.

Luke answered his phone, his stomach turning over as the voice on the other end of the line said, 'G'day mate. Milo here. It's time we had a little talk. '